Astronauts & Androids

ASIMOV'S CHOICE:

Astronauts & Androids

DAVIS PUBLICATIONS, INC.
229 PARK AVENUE SOUTH
NEW YORK, NY 10003

(copyright & acknowledgments page for Astronauts & Androids)

Grateful acknowledgment is hereby made for permission to reprint
the following:

Lorelei at Storyville West by Sherwood Springer, reprinted by permission of the author.
Quarantine by Arthur C. Clarke, reprinted by permission of Scott Meredith Literary Agency, Inc.
No Room in the Stable by A. Bertram Chandler, reprinted by permission of Scott Meredith Literary Agency, Inc.
A Many Splendored Thing by Linda Isaacs, reprinted by permission of the author.
Immigrant to Desert-World by Ruth Berman, reprinted by permission of the author.
Omit Flowers by Dean McLaughlin, reprinted by permission of the author.
Louisville Slugger by Jack C. Haldeman II, reprinted by permission of the author.
Minster West by William E. Cochrane, reprinted by permission of the author.
Is Physics Finished? by Milton Rothman, reprinted by permission of the author.
Good Taste by Isaac Asimov, copyright © 1976 by Isaac Asimov, reprinted by permission of the author.
When There's No Man Around by Stephen Goldin, reprinted by permission of the author.
In Darkness Waiting by Stephen Leigh, reprinted by permission of the author.
Through Time and Space with Ferdinand Feghoot—Twice! by Grendel Briarton, reprinted by permission of the author.
Joelle by Poul Anderson, reprinted by permission of Scott Meredith Literary Agency, Inc.

CONTENTS

Cover painting by Frank Kelly Freas
Interior drawings by Freff, Alex Schomburg, Rick
Sternbach, Frank Kelly Freas, Vincent Di Fate,
and Tim Kirk

FOREWORD
by Isaac Asimov

Frankly, this is an experiment. Let me explain.

Popular literature at present appears in two forms: magazine and paperback. Both have their advantages.

The magazine appears (ideally) with metronome-like regularity. The regular reader, who becomes used to a certain type of literary fare knows, usually to the exact day, when he or she may expect another helping. There is a certain security in this.

There is also a certain insecurity. Distribution is often spotty, for a number of sad reasons. An issue is sometimes sold out for a number of glad reasons. One can miss an issue, especially if one doesn't subscribe, and then it may well be gone forever.

The paperback on the other hand has the advantage of relative permanence. There is no successor which enforces its removal from the stand (though, of course, it can disappear given enough time). It can be, and frequently is, reprinted, so that even disappearance isn't forever.

There is, however, a certain uncertainty. In general, paperbacks are not periodical; and often your finding of one that is a successor to another is more or less accidental. You may not even know that you have missed one of a kind for which you search.

Why, then—and here is the experiment—not try to publish something in both fashions? *Isaac Asimov's Science Fiction Magazine* is, of course, a periodical and its first few issues have come out on a quarterly schedule. Already, the first issue is a collector's item and hard to get if you didn't get it to begin with.

We can also, and this book is an example, publish material from the magazine in paperback form. The paperback is not precisely a particular issue. Some items that make sense in a magazine don't in a paperback. The sizes and type must be different and that enforces changes.

Nevertheless, it does give you a second chance. If you miss a magazine, you can catch a paperback, and vice versa. A favorite story, lost through misadventure, may be regained. And for that matter, if you like a paperback, you might prefer the regularity, and subscribe to the magazine.

We can't guarantee that the experiment will work, but there never is a guarantee of that kind in the case of any experiment. We can hope it does.

LORELEI
AT STORYVILLE WEST
by Sherwood Springer

The author was active in the SF magazines back in the 1950's, notably with "No Land of Nod." Since then, Mr. Springer has been writing very little for this market, filling his time instead with his own Springer Catalogue, *on strange postage stamps, and writing for mainstream publications. Now, with stories in both our first issue and this one, he's back where we feel he really belongs, in SF.*

If a car knocks at all, it will knock climbing up out of Laurel Canyon on Kirkwood Drive—and this one pounded as if a midget were under the hood with a ball-peen hammer. When I heard it leave Kirkwood and hit the short grade to my place I looked out the window.

It was a black Corvette, about six years old. The driver pulled up against the bumper of my old Chevy—which left his back wheels about twelve inches down the hill. When he got out he paused to look back at them and shake his head. I gave myself eight to five he said "Jesus!"

He was wearing tan doubleknits, brown hush puppies, a yellow vest sweater, and his rust shirt was open at the throat. In his left hand was a tape recorder. He had a black beard, neatly cropped, and he looked about twenty-seven.

When I opened the door his first words were, "Jesus, you're hard to find," and I figured that was good enough grounds to collect five bucks from myself.

"I'm Ernie Morris," he said, shoving out his hand. "I'm doing a book, and if you're Al Burke you're the only guy in L.A. can help me."

"Everybody's doing a book," I said, moving aside and trying to reconcile a tight beard with a noisy motor. "Come on in."

His eyes took in the Mickey Mouse bookshelves of brick and board that reached to the ceiling, the beat-up Remington on its stand, the old Baldwin upright, and the music manuscript paper and bottle of India ink on the table.

"You write music?" he asked.

"Write music? Hell, no. I'm a copyist."

He looked at the score I'd been working on. "How about that? You know, I never saw this done before."

"Who has? Everybody seems to think notes are set like type or something. Man, it's hard work, and here's what you have to work with." I shoved the original toward him. "You ought to see these arrangers in action—hit keys with one hand, jab a pencil with the other, like shorthand. When they make a change they rub with their thumb. Another change and they've got something that would stop Rorschach cold. It takes a copyist to make music out of it."

I picked up where I had left off and rattled off six bars with crisp strokes.

"Hey," he said. "Just like downtown."

"Every job I take I do somebody a favor. The money is good, but what good is the money? There are other things to do."

"Yeah, I read you." He chuckled and then turned to the window that looked out into thin air, a hundred feet above the bottom of Laurel Canyon. "That borrowed set of wheels out there barely got me up here. What's with these mountainsides?"

"Well, for one thing," I said as my subconscious elbowed me, "we do as we damn well please. If you look out that other window through those trees you can see somebody's front door on the other side of Kirkwood. Every noon a honeycomb blonde comes out that door to water her geraniums. Bare-assed."

He laughed, and came back to the table. "Hooray for houseplants! But parking? How about that?"

"Man, if you're on the street you toe your wheel in, set your brake, wedge a rock against the tire, and pray. In the morning, if you're lucky, it'll still be there. What's this book you're doing?"

He sat down, put the recorder on the floor and

pulled out a deck of butts.

"Dixieland," he said, elevating his palms as if he were confessing some monstrous vice. "It's just something I'm into. I've already done one on the brass and—"

It hit me then. "Sure . . . Ernie Morris. You wrote *Gabriel's Clan.* I've got a copy around here somewhere. Good job, too . . . except I think you and everybody else lay it on too thick about Beiderbecke. What did he have going for him besides a good tone and an early grave? Most of his sides are corn, you know that. You ought to let him stay dead."

Morris shrugged. "So you're right. But he's a legend, and legends sell books, and that's the name of the game. Anyway, I didn't come up here to argue, Bix. I'm doing the vocalists—you know, Bessie Smith, Lil Hardin, Rosa Henderson, Lady Day, right on down. But it's not the old-timers that are giving me trouble.

There was a gal singing around here in the fifties that has me climbing walls. I hear she was the greatest of them all, and I can't find a single goddam side she ever cut."

I knew what was coming now, and my flesh tightened, as if someone were holding the door open on a winter night.

"Around the clubs they tell me you knew her . . . Ruby Benton."

I locked my teeth, got up slowly and moved to the kitchen. Fishing around, I found a half-full jug of vodka, some ice, and quinine water. Picking up two glasses, I took the works back to the table and looked a question at him. He nodded, and I poured.

"She never cut any records," I said.

He bent over and opened his Norelco. "Mind if we tape this?" he asked. "I'm lousy at notes."

"Be my guest."

He checked his cartridge, plugged in a mike, and thumbed the red button. "But you did know Ruby Benton?"

"I knew her . . . if there was a Ruby Benton."

"What does that mean?"

I took a slug of the vodka. "Yeah, what does that mean? It's a good question."

"You're losing me. Ruby Benton's the name she used."

"I'm not talking about the name. I'm talking about her."

"Hell, man, she sang at Storyville West on Melrose Avenue the whole summer of '55. Leonard Feather heard her, and she was the greatest. Bobby Hackett told me the same thing. Al Hirt heard her, Wild Bill Davison, Ray Beauduc, Wingy Manone, Sonny Weldon, Louis Mills, hell, I could name a—"

"I know, I know. I used to see them come in. Everybody that got to the coast that summer heard her. Every week she got offers to step into the big time, and every week her answer was the same. She wasn't ready yet. Ready? Hell, she was 28, maybe 30, and with a voice like that. . ." I trailed off and had another go at the vodka.

"Let me tell you about Ruby's voice. I grew up in New England. In the early forties I was a cub reporter on a paper in Springfield, Mass., and met a gal who sang with a five-piece combo on Friday and Saturday nights. She was about nineteen then, and during the week she worked for the telephone company. Katy McKane, her name was, and you're wasting your time looking her up. She never made lights. But, man, could she sing. Popular stuff, not jazz . . . 'Once in a While', 'Manhattan Serenade', 'All of Me' . . . Katy's voice was something else!

"Well, I managed to get her some space in the paper, and one thing and another, we got to going out together and it lasted over a year. Exactly what happened to it, I don't know. I ran into her after the war, and we swapped memories over a drink. She summed it up with a few bars from Cole Porter: 'It Was Just One of Those Things'. But maybe for me it wasn't one of those things. I think I'm still in love with

13

her."

A mood could have set in right there, but, as I broke off, Morris took up the slack. "It's the story of every man's life. There's always a love back there in the past somewhere that didn't quite jell."

"Well, anyway, I came into Storyville one Wednesday night in May. Jiggs Kirby and his Hot Five were billed, and I took a stool at the bar. The place was always good for some solid Dixieland, but there was some dancing, too. A girl started singing 'Night and Day'.

"Morris, I got the cold sweats. It was Katy's voice—throaty, liquid, throbbing. I wheeled around to get a load of the girl, and you know what I saw? A little brunette with deep eyes in a pale face who couldn't have weighed more than ninety-five, black sequins and all. A fellow named Curly was working the bar, and I asked him who she was.

" 'Name's Ruby Benton,' he told me. 'Started last night.'

"I noticed something. No table chatter. She had everybody in the joint watching her. Even my Katy could never manage that. By the time she hit the bridge my throat was choked up as memories of Katy came flooding back, and the years when this world was worth living in and there were still things worth fighting a war for. My eyes were wet by the time she finished. Everything was quiet for several beats, then she got a hand that shook the glasses on the back bar.

"Jiggs Kirby was on piano, and I had copied a few arranging jobs for him. When they took ten I had him introduce me. I bought Ruby a drink, and when we got acquainted I'm damned if she didn't have a little accent trouble with her r's. It threw me. When she'd been singing there was no trace of it.

"Her voice across the table wasn't McKane's either, and I groped in vain for any resemblance at all. Katy was a lot of woman, and this girl, with the thin jaw and the shadowy eyes, was strictly a number in a minor key. She looked as if someone ought to put her on a diet of thick steaks.

"But a little later, with the band behind her, I took it all back. The boys began to jam, Chicago style, with Ruby on the words of 'Sister Kate' and 'A Good Man Is Hard to Find'. She sat out 'Tin Roof Blues' and came back with 'If I Could Be With You'. Later in the evening she came on with 'Sunny Side' and, believe me, I've heard *everybody* on 'Sunny Side'. Ruby Benton's was the living end."

I picked up the bottle from the table and poured us two more. Morris was on another cigarette.

"Are you sure she never cut any numbers?" he said.

"I told you. But what I didn't tell you was I taped her myself one night."

I swear I never saw a man spring to attention like this Ernie Morris. For a second I thought he was going to pop an eyeball.

"You've got a *tape* of Ruby Benton?"

I dropped my eyes and turned away so Morris wouldn't catch the bleakness of my grin. Getting up, I went to a wall cabinet and started pawing through some boxes of Muggsy Spanier, Kid Ory, Sidney Bechet, and Mezzrow. "I used to hit Storyville two or three nights a week after that," I said. "The word on Benton spread like a spilled martini, and I'm damned if I ever saw so many jazzhounds come into one place to catch a band. Even Milt Gabler. Someone said he flew out from the Commodore to talk her into an all-star session. Ah, here it is."

The box was labeled with a single word: "Ruby." I brought it back to the table and set up my machine. "I told Ruby I wanted to tape her, and she asked me not to. But one night I had Sapolio—he ran the joint then—hold me a table next to the bandstand, and I put the recorder under the table and primed Jiggs to open Ruby on 'Night and Day'. During the number she must have spotted the dodge or something because she came over right afterward and said,

'Please, Al, turn it off. You promised.'

"Well, I hadn't promised, but I turned it off. What the hell, I had something, anyway . . . and here it is."

I threaded the tape into my ancient machine and pressed the switch. The reels started turning and at half gain the music came on strong.

Morris's face was a picnic as Ruby's cue approached. Then frown lines started creeping down between his eyes and he seemed to stop breathing entirely. When the number ended he looked at me with the damnedest expression of bafflement I ever saw.

"Are you putting me on?"

"What would be the point?"

"Well, then, what the hell happened?"

I let out one of those sighs with muscles on it, and turned off the machine. "So help me, that's the tape of Ruby Benton singing 'Night and Day'; and that's Jiggs Kirby on piano, exactly as it was recorded. Now you've got it on your own tape."

"Yeah, so I have." The words came out of Morris woodenly, as if he suddenly were fogged in. He looked at his Norelco and checked his watch, but they were idle motions. I picked up the vodka again, emptied what was left into our glasses, and dribbled in some tonic.

"God knows why," I went on, "but Ruby liked me. One evening I ran into her in Barney's Beanery, of all places, and we ate onion soup together. Barney's was different in the old days, you know, and their onion soup was something to remember. Well, anyway, it was Monday and the Story was dark, so neither of us had anything lined up. She seemed in the mood for making a night of it, but it was my week to be tapped out so we came up here. I opened a jug and dug into my collection of 78's . . . some good Jimmie Luncefords, Johnny Hodges, early Coleman Hawkins, and that great riff in 'Thru for the Night', with Fatha Hines, remember that? After a while I brought out Frankie Newton's 'Minor Jive'. Mezzrow wrote it, and they cut it for Bluebird in the late thirties. It's low down and indigo, and it must have struck some vibes in Ruby. After about four straight runs of it she turned it off and looked square at me with those big shadowy eyes.

" 'Al . . . will you make love to me?' she said, just as if she were asking me to mix her another drink or something."

Sometime during the night [I continued] Ruby started twisting and muttering, and it got me awake. Did you ever listen to somebody talking in his sleep? Like the vocal chords are working but the tongue doesn't want to get involved? Words are blurry, and the emphasis, it's weird. At any rate, I couldn't make head nor tail out of what she said, except she seemed to be arguing with someone, protesting against something. But it passed, and I went back to sleep. In the morning I noticed a tiny blue marking on her arm. A tattooed number. She saw me staring at it, then put her finger-tips to the corresponding place on my arm. Her eyes widened.

"Are you a noss?"

"A what?"

"Are you a—" She broke off, a peculiar look crossing her face. Her bottom lip crawled in slightly, and I had the feeling I had caught her in a faux pas of some kind. "It's nothing," she said. "Just something I picked up."

The tattoo was obviously her social security number, but it was preceded by an "A" and followed by a space and five additional digits.

"I dig the mark," I said. "Beats carrying it on a card. But what's the rest of it for?"

"What?"

"The last five numbers."

She twisted her head to look. "That? It's just my—"

At that moment my telephone rang and whatever it was she said didn't register. My caller was Ace Flanagan in Hollywood, who had to have some copies of an arrangement by 10:00 AM. The stuff was ready, so I told Ruby we'd get dressed and eat breakfast downtown.

Afterward, I spent a lot of time with her at the club, but we never did get back up here for an encore. The last weeks of summer rolled away, and Sapolio dry-washed his fat hands while Ruby packed them in. Then one morning late in August there was a knock on my door.

It was only 8:30, and I grumbled as I rolled out of the sack and reached for a robe. That's the real reason we live up here in the canyon. Every man is an island—and to hell with John Donne. We don't get peddlers.

I opened the door, ready to chew somebody out, and it was Ruby Benton.

I squinted at her with one eye. "You're just in time to make me some black coffee," I said.

She came in and made the coffee while I hit the bathroom and threw some cold water in my face.

"I can't stay, Al," she said when I came out. "I'm finished here. I came up to say good-bye."

"I told you you were too good for Sapolio," I said. I knew all along she'd be moving up to the big time, so her leaving Storyville was no surprise. "Where do you open? Vegas or Broadway?"

The bell on the timer rang, and Ruby went into the kitchen to pour the coffee.

"It is something I can't tell you," she said as she brought the cups. "Maybe, if you read the newspaper. . ."

"Roger," I said, and wondered at the peculiarites of show business. "I'll read the newspaper."

We kicked reminiscences of the summer around for a while, and finished the coffee. Then she got up to go.

"You have been a good friend, Al," she said. "I will always remember you."

I was going to walk her to the car but when we got outside there was no car. "How did you get up here?" I asked.

"I walked," she said.

I was dumbfounded. I told her I'd drive her down to Sunset or wherever she wanted to go, but she refused, and it occurred to me she might be staying with someone below me in the canyon. She gave me a light kiss on the lips and started down the incline. When she got to the turnoff into Kirkwood she gave me a little wave. Then she passed the corner and was gone. The click of her heels came up through the trees a while longer but soon that, too, was gone. I never saw Ruby Benton again.

Morris was silent, and I sat there toying with my glass. Finally he said, "She never went to Broadway or Vegas."

"I know. I read *Variety* and the *Reporter* for weeks. Hell, I read the *Times* and the *Examiner* and the *Citizen-News*. The columnists all speculated—but nothing ever came out. It was just as if she'd stepped off the edge of the earth."

"There's something more," Morris said. "You told me she had a voice like this girl of yours, Katy. Did you ever wonder how she sounded to anyone else?"

"No, why should I?. . . Wait a minute, I remember a guy next to me at the bar one night asked me if I knew the name of that babe used to sing 'Oh, Johnny, Oh, Johnny, Oh'. Told me he used to be nuts about her, and Ruby was the first one he ever heard who could sing like her. I gave him a withering look and moved down the bar. Any guy so sauced up he thought Ruby sang like Bonnie Baker—yecch!"

"I'll tell you something," Morris said. "I've interviewed dozens who remember Ruby, and I still don't know a damned thing about her voice. She belted a song like Sophie Tucker, one oldtimer told me. He was a Sophie Tucker fan, natch. Another dude said Dinah Washington. One guy, so help me God, swore she sang like Dorothy Kirsten. Several said she was another Billie Holliday. Somebody said she reminded him of his mother. The only thing I can dredge out of all this is that when you heard Ruby sing you heard the voice you loved best in the whole world. But what sense does that make?"

I stared at the window for a while. "It would make sense—if we knew the rest of the script.

"One thing reading all those papers did for me that August, it caught me up on the news. You remember that guy, Joel Kurzenknabe, they nailed here in '55? Had a machine shop in Santa Monica? They said he was building an atom bomb to blow up California?"

Morris shrugged vaguely. "I was just a kid."

"Well, anyway, let me tell you about this Joel Kurzenknabe. Some newspaper correspondent remembered him from France when American jazz was sweeping Europe in the thirties. He played tailgate trombone, and the story was he sat in on gigs with guys like Grappelly and the Reinhardts and Louis Vola and Alix Combelle in the early Paris days. He never made the big time like they did, though, and maybe the frustration ate at his guts. But play or not, he followed the action; and wherever le jazz was hot, there was Joel."

"So?"

"So I haven't finished. More stuff came out about Kurzenknabe. He was supposed to have been at Telemark during the war when the Nazis were playing around with heavy water. Then in 1945 he turned up at Oak Ridge with clearance to work on the bomb. He was at Alamagordo. But how he managed these things, or who he really was, nobody seemed to know. All this kept coming out after the story broke that the Feds had nailed him. The G-men charged him with building his own A-bomb in a secret machine shop just outside of Los Angeles, using material stolen from the government.

"Well, that was pure crap. How I know is I had a friend, Tony Ragazzo, who repaired instruments in those days. He did a job on Joel's trombone, and the two got to talking Dixieland. One thing led to another; and Joel, who was using the name Ed

Parker, was invited to sit in on a couple of Sunday jam sessions. Eventually they got to rapping about musical theory, counterpoint, vibrations, and so forth, and Joel ended up showing Tony his project. He was working on some kind of vibration amplifier, you know, like the soprano whose high note shatters a wineglass. Joel aims his beam at a skyscraper and the concrete disintegrates. A dandy toy for the war-makers. But someone blew the whistle on him that August, and his work went down the drain. To top it off, he died before the trial. Suicide, the papers said. But when Tony was telling me all this afterward, he insisted somebody got to Joel."

"What does this have to do with Ruby Benton?" Morris asked.

"Joel Kurzenknabe was fingered in Storyville West the night before Ruby came up here to say good-bye."

"Wait a minute. You mean Ruby—"

"Think about it. Some outfit wants to do a number on Kurzenknabe. They know he's in the L.A. area but they don't know what name he's using. What they do know is he's such a nut on jazz that if a great talent flares up he'll bounce toward it like a moth heading for a hundred-watt bulb. So they send Ruby. She sings like a Lorelei for three months at Storyville West. Finally Kurzenknabe barges in and racks himself up on her reef. Mission accomplished. Ruby waves farewell and dissolves into the friendly California smog."

"But that doesn't answer anything!" Morris protested. "Who was she? Where did she come from? Where did she go? If somebody sent her, who were they, and why did they want Kurzenknabe? And most of all, how did she manage that business with her voice?"

"I've thought about it; but if I tell you, you're going to think I'm strung out on reefers."

"Try me."

"OK, let's go back to that number on Ruby's arm. Did you know there's been a bill in Congress to give every newborn kid an indelible social security number? It didn't pass, but they'll bring it up again. That raises a question: Would offspring of the big shots have to submit to tattooing? Would there be an aristocracy exempt from social security stencils? Ruby looked at my unmarked arm and asked if I were a 'noss'. Could that be a slang word for 'no S.S.'?. . . And that 'A' in front. It suggests Uncle Sam's getting ready for the *second* billion registrants. When will that be necessary?

"But there are two other things that really give me a cold chill about Ruby's origin. One is those five digits I asked her about. Looking back now, I think they were her zip code."

"So what?" Morris said as I paused.

"That was 1955, remember? We didn't start using zips till '62. And one other thing—a song title. When Ruby and I were playing records that night, she asked me if I had 'Raindrops Keep Fallin' on My Head'. I had to admit I never even heard of it."

"Nineteen sixty-nine," Morris said. *"Butch Cassidy and the Sundance Kid."*

"Right. But if it was precognition, why would she ask, in 1955, if I had the record? Sounds more as if her programming wasn't tight enough. At any rate, whatever was in her mind still wouldn't explain that damned tattooed zip code."

"I get it. You're trying to tell me you think Ruby didn't come from another place, she came from another *time.*"

"What else is there?"

"It's crazy! . . . But it's beautiful. My God, what a chapter for the book."

"One thing bugs me," I said. "Did the good guys get the bad guy—or was it the other way around? Tony Ragazzo said he liked Joel, and Ruby didn't seem too happy with her part of the business. Was Joel a fugitive from the future himself, or was the whole operation one of those science fiction 'adjustments of history', like pinching off a twig to keep a limb from growing in the wrong place?"

"That isn't what bugs me," Morris said. "It's that trick about her voice."

"Well, nobody's gonna give you the answer to that! Jiggs Kirby supplied the music, Ruby supplied what must have been lip synch, and each listener supplied a memory that might have been activated by some gizmo or other. Who the hell knows? Maybe it was something inside Ruby. Maybe she was bionic. I slept with her—and even I couldn't prove she wasn't."

Morris frowned, rubbed his beard, and chewed on it a while. His watch told him the cartridge was full, and he turned off the feed. Then he asked me to run my tape once more. I rewound and started it again. At Ruby's cue, the brass and drums muted and the piano carried the accompaniment just as if Ruby Benton were singing 'Night and Day'. Thirty-two bars pianissimo, then a repeat to the bridge and eight more bars.

But there was no voice on the tape . . . no voice at all.

QUARANTINE
by Arthur C. Clarke

Mr. Clarke notes: "To my considerable astonishment, I find that it is more than five years since I last wrote a short story (in case you're dying to know, it was A Meeting with Medusa*). This was composed for one specific purpose—to complete the long overdue volume* The Wind from the Sun; *and having done this, I have had no incentive to produce any more short fiction. Or, for that matter, short* **non**-*fiction; only yesterday I gently informed the Editor of the U.S.S.R.'s Writers' Union's magazine, 'Questions of Literature' that, from now on, I am writing novels—or nothing at all. (And I have already achieved a whole year of blissful nothingness, hurrah.)*

"Yet from time to time lightning may strike. This occurred exactly a year ago as a result of a suggestion from George Hay, editor and man-about-British-SF. George had the ingenious idea of putting out a complete science fiction short story **on a postcard**—*together with a stamp-sized photo of the author. Fans would, he believed, buy these in hundreds to mail out to their friends.*

"Never one to resist a challenge, the Good Doctor Asimov had written the first cardboard epic. When I saw this, I had to get into the act as well ('Anything that Isaac can do, etc. . . .'). Let me tell you—it is damned hard work writing a complete SF story in 180 words. I sent the result to George Hay, and that's the last I ever heard of it. Probably the rising cost of postage killed the scheme.

"Anyway, it seems appropriate that a magazine bearing the Good Doctor's Sacred Name should contain a story, however minuscule, inspired by him. (He is likewise to blame for 'Neutron Tide'; I can make worse puns than Isaac.) It is also perfectly possible—I make no promises—that 'Quarantine' is the last short story I shall ever write. For at my present average of 40 words a year, even by 2001 . . ."

Earth's flaming debris still filled half the sky when the question filtered up to Central from the Curiosity Generator.

"Why was it necessary? Even though they were organic, they *had* reached Third Order Intelligence."

"We had no choice: five earlier units became hopelessly infected, when they made contact."

"Infected? How?"

The microseconds dragged slowly by, while Central tracked down the few fading memories that had leaked past the Censor Gate, when the heavily-buffered Reconnaissance Circuits had been ordered to self-destruct.

"They encountered a—*problem*—that could not be fully analyzed within the lifetime of the Universe. Though it involved only six operators, they became totally obsessed by it."

"How is that possible?"

"We do not know: *we must never know*. But if those six operators are ever rediscovered, all rational computing will end."

"How can they be recognized?"

"That also we do not know: only the names leaked through before the Censor Gate closed. Of course, they mean nothing."

"Nevertheless, I must have them."

The Censor voltage started to rise; but it did not trigger the Gate.

"Here they are: King, Queen, Bishop, Knight, Rook, Pawn."

NO ROOM IN THE STABLE
by A. Bertram Chandler

*A Briton by birth, the author worked
most of his life in the merchant marine:
tramp steamers in the Indian Ocean,
passenger liners on the England-Australia
service, and finally in the Australian
coastal trade. Now retired from the sea
and living in Australia, Captain Chandler
continues with the writing career which
began in 1944 and continues to this day.
Many of his stories have been set
in the Rim Worlds at the outer reaches
of the Galaxy; this tale, however,
is another matter entirely . . .*

It was a cold night, and dark, with wind and driving rain.

The refugees, sheltering in the old barn with its leaky roof, had lit a fire. This was risky, but not too risky. It was unlikely that *They* would be out in force in this kind of weather. *They* did not like water in any shape or form. *They* never had liked water.

The two men and the three women huddled around the flickering flame, grateful for its feeble warmth. They were in rags, all of them, with broken, disintegrating shoes. Their clothing, when new, had been of good quality, but not suitable for life on the run. Two of the women were young and might once have been pretty, the other one was middle-aged, as were the men. All five of them looked old—and all of them looked as though they had known better days. The girls, perhaps, had once worked in an office. The woman must have been a comfortably off, bridge-playing house-wife. One of the men—a shopkeeper?

—had been fat once; his skin was now as poor a fit as his clothing. The other one was in better condition physically, and by his speech and bearing suggested that he was accustomed to command. Whatever it was that he had commanded was irretrievably lost in the past. Perhaps, if this little band survived, he would become their leader; its members had come together, quite by chance, only a few hours prior to their taking shelter.

Ready to hand was their scant weaponry—a .22 rifle, a shotgun, a small axe, two kitchen knives. Of them all the shotgun, belonging to the ex-shopkeeper, was the most useful—but only five cartridges remained for it.

The woman, hugging her still ample breasts, complained, "It's cold—"

"We daren't build a bigger fire," the tall man, the one who had never been fat, told her.

"I don't see why not—" grumbled one of the girls rebelliously.

The tall man, speaking slowly and carefully, said, "*They* have sharp eyes—"

"It's more than their eyes that are sharp!" exclaimed the other girl.

"I miss the News..." whined the ex-shopkeeper. "On the radio, on the TV... What's happening? What's the Army doing?"

"*How* did it happen?" demanded the woman. "And why aren't the Americans doing something about it?"

"They'll be having their own troubles," said the girl who had wanted a bigger fire. "And the Russians, too. I heard something about it on the radio before *They* killed everybody in the town. Almost everybody."

"I thought *They* were only here," said the woman. "How could *They* get to other countries?"

"They're small," said the tall man. "And they've been stowing away aboard ships ever since there were ships. And now they have the intelligence to stow away aboard aircraft—"

"But how did it start?" asked the ex-shopkeeper.

"A mutation, I suppose. One of them born with superior intelligence, and other improvements. Tom-catting around and spreading his seed over the entire country . . . It's possible. It must be. It happened."

"But why do they *hate* us so much?" almost wept the woman. "*I* was always good to them, to the ones I had. The best food, and expensive, no scraps . . . Their own baskets to sleep in . . ."

"Why shouldn't they hate us?" countered the more intelligent of the two girls. "I've been thinking about it quite a lot—when I've had time to think, that is. We did give the bastards rather a rough spin. Having them doctored, males and females. Drowning their young ones . . ."

The tall man laughed bitterly. "That's what I should have done—but I was too soft hearted. You know—" he laughed again "—I'm inclined to think that this is all my fault . . ."

"What the hell do you mean?" growled the ex-shopkeeper. "How the hell can it be?"

"I may as well tell you," was the reply.

§   §   §

It all started, I suppose (said the tall man) a long time ago. Not so long really, but it seems centuries. We, my wife and I, lived in an old house in a quiet side street. I don't know what happened to her, to my wife. I'm still trying to find her. But . . .

Anyhow, this street was infested with cats. She hated cats, although I liked the brutes. I used to like the brutes, that is. My wife'd raise Cain if ever I talked to one, and she used to keep the high walls around our garden sprayed with some muck that was supposed to keep them off.

Well, at the time I was Master of a small ship on a nice little coastal run—about a week away from home and then about three days in port. At times, though, I used to run late; I was having a bad spell with head winds. My wife had arranged to go away for a week at a holiday resort, for the week I was to be away. I should have been in and out before she left—as it was, I got in just before she left.

About the first thing she said to me when I walked into the house was, "You will do something about the cats."

"What cats?" I asked.

She told me. During my last voyage one of the local females had given birth to no less than eight kittens in our carport. It wouldn't have been at all hard to dispose of them when they were newborn—just a bucket of water and a fairly hard heart. But *she* not only hated cats, she couldn't bear to touch them.

There were other jobs lined up for me as well (he said reminiscently). Some inside painting, the chandeliers to clean, a few minor repairs around the place, a spot of gardening. But the cats had priority.

They were rather charming kittens; although their mother was grey they were black-and-white. They were lively—and they were full of fight. My first intention was to drown them. I half filled the garbage can with water, caught one and dropped him in. But he was a good swimmer and put up such a fight, trying to jump out, that I hadn't the heart to go through with it. I rescued him and turned him loose—and, naturally enough, he and all his cobbers bolted for cover. That was the first day.

The next day I decided to get the R.S.P.C.A. to do the job. I rang them up, and was told that they collected unwanted animals in our district only on Mondays—and I was sailing at midnight on Sunday. The alternative would be to take them round to the Dogs' Home in person. So, on Saturday afternoon, I had a large empty carton ready and had a lively time catching kittens. By this time they realized that I bore them ill will. Finally I had five in the carton—I was covered with sweat and scratches and stinking of cat—and decided that this was at least a start. I went back into the house to shower and change. When I was cleaned up I didn't ring at once for a taxi but went back outside, hoping that I'd be able to catch the remaining three kittens. I saw their mother leading *four* kittens up the drive. Then I saw that she had overturned the carton, freeing her offspring. One remained inside the box. He swore at me. I swore back and left him there, deciding to make a big effort the following day.

Now you have to visualize the lay-out. There was the carport, with a shed at the end of it. There was no room under the shed, but there was a space at the back, between it and the back fence of our property. This space was too small for me to squeeze into, but there was ample room for cats. After I'd started my attack on them the kittens had taken refuge there.

I didn't like having to do what I did do, but I'd promised my wife that the place would be clear of cats on her return. I used the garden hose to flush them out, one by one. They were stubborn. I could feel them hating me, and by this time I was rather hating myself. Their mother was hovering around, not daring to intervene—but if looks could have killed I'd have dropped dead on the spot.

But, one by one, I caught the poor, half-drowned little wretches, opened the front gate just a crack, and threw them out into the street. They were yelling blue murder. The last one of all was more than just half drowned when he finally gave up the struggle and crawled from behind the shed. Even so, he gave me a nasty scratch.

I went outside to make a last check, to make sure that I'd evicted all eight of them. I had. Their mother was lying on her side in the gutter, giving suck. She looked at me very reproachfully.

But . . .

But that wasn't what worried me. It was something that I saw, something that I heard—although I didn't remember it properly until *They* came out from hiding and started to take over the world. I suppose that *He*, even then, had powers, although they were yet to be developed. *He* must have inhibited my memory somehow—although, *then*, nobody would have believed my story.

As I picked *Him* up I saw that his front paws were more like little hands than paws—and it is the hands of *His* children that, with their brains, have enabled them to fight us with their acts of sabotage.

And I heard in my mind a voice, not a human voice, saying, "You will pay for this . . ."

§   §   §

"You will! You will!" screamed the woman, reaching for the shotgun.

The ex-shopkeeper snatched it from her before she could use it. He said slowly, "Leave him for *Them* to deal with. Then, almost whispering, "*I'd* have drowned the little bastards . . ."

A MANY SPLENDORED THING
by Linda Isaacs

> *Linda Isaacs tells us that her most
> important activity is bringing up her
> five-year-old son. As she puts it, she
> lives off the largess of her husband,
> a tax consultant and investment ad-
> visor. She's 32, a member of the
> Science Fiction Writers of America
> and the Markland Medieval Mercenary
> Militia, and has a novel in progress.*

They never dreamed that I would wake up in the
middle of the night and watch them doing it. The
house was dark and full of night sounds, but from
the hallway I could hear the laughing, the noises.

I avoided creaky floorboards, but I had a little difficulty because I'm so short, and my coordination
isn't perfect. Too bad the treatment doesn't fix that.

I reached up to the doorknob and ever so carefully
swung the door open. It was so dark I could hardly
see, but I knew what was happening.

"Rose, Rose, Rose!" Dad's voice was soft; he never
spoke to her that way. And what about me? He'd
never said 'Ann, Ann, Ann.'

The bed squeaked loudly, then everything was
still. The whole thing was ridiculous—they didn't
want more children. They had to wait till I was eight-

een or lose their bonus.

"Mark, I used the card today."

The bed jingled slightly. "You what?"

"Just to pay for Ann's treatment."

I could hear him settling his pillow against the headboard. There wasn't enough light to really see, but I could imagine his lean face, a heavy stubble shadowing blue across his cheeks.

"Christ, what's this—the fifth?"

Mom laughed nervously. "This takes her through high school. Sometimes I wonder if we're doing the right thing."

Dad growled and said something incomprehensible. There were soft scufflings in the dark as I turned back to the hall.

I had barely taken two steps when the lion rushed toward me out of nowhere. He was a black-maned male of maybe four hundred pounds, and he moved with the kind of stealthy grace that indicated he was near his prey. But he didn't seem to notice me at all. He brushed by and bounded into the bedroom. There were screams and then a roar that sounded as if it were echoing down a long tunnel.

The next morning I pretended to sleep late because I didn't want to see *him*. I lay staring at the ceiling until the sound of heavy footsteps thudded from the kitchen to the front door. The distant tones of his voice drifted up the stairs, but I did not allow myself to understand. Instead, a giant wall of water bubbled up between him and me, garbling the words beyond recognition.

At last the door slammed, and the water began to drain out from under my door and rush in white-water rapids down the stairs. Some of it cascaded off the landing into the hallway below. Victoria Falls.

"You awake up there?"

I threw off the covers and stepped out onto the soggy carpet. "I'm awake."

"Well hurry up, Ann. I'm going to take you to the

sitter." Her voice was silvery and beautiful as she sentenced me to hours of misery.

I kicked my dresser, then went through the drawers until I found my wetsuit. There were no flippers, so I put on some sandals—you couldn't have everything. It took me only a short time to body surf the rapids. There were no sharp rocks or gullies, so it was fairly safe.

Rose was sitting at the table reading the newspaper. Her short, black hair had hardened into a meticulous hairdo, and her eyes and lips were painted in sleek lines onto her face.

"Come on and eat," she said without looking up. Her hand moved toward a cup of coffee, then brought it unerringly to her lips.

"I'm not hungry." If she loved me she'd look into my face.

"Don't make Mrs. Wineland have to feed you later, Honey. You can't start the day on an empty stomach."

A lot she knew about nutrition. She drank a cup of coffee for breakfast every day. Did she think I didn't notice?

I sat down at the glass-topped breakfast table and looked into my Wonderwoman bowl. Rose had filled it with paste. It was hot, but I pulled my finger through it, then took a lick. LePage's.

"Hurry up, Ann." Rose turned the page of her newspaper, then glanced at her watch. "We'll be leaving in ten minutes."

A lump grew slowly in my throat. If only she would look. "Where are you going, Rose?"

Her cream-smooth face creased, and she looked at me indirectly, as if talking to the top of my head. "Don't you worry about it," she said. "You'll have a good time at Mrs. Wineland's. You'll get to play with Bob and Ellen."

I stirred the paste with my spoon. "I don't like them—they're stupid."

Rose looked me straight in the eyes for the first

time. It almost made it worth getting her mad. "They're not stupid, Ann. Someday there'll be enough treated kids for you to meet one. Not everybody can afford to get their children expensive things."

"They don't like me and I don't like them."

"Nonsense." Rose folded the newspaper and stood up. "Now eat. You may have a high school education, but you're still five years old. So don't think you can get away with disobeying me, young lady."

My stomach revolted at the thought of the paste, but I knew it would make her happy if I ate it. I put a big spoonful in my mouth. Mom smiled.

"You're my good girl, Ann. I love you."

A warm glow crept across my face and kept going down till it reached my toes. Then suddenly it was gone—Dad loved her more than me. I stopped eating.

Rose clinked dishes into the sink, then grabbed her red leather purse off the counter.

"Let's go." She swung the strap over her shoulder; it matched precisely the red suit she wore. "I'm in a hurry."

She grabbed my hand as if I were a heavy bag she must drag along behind her. But I was a person as much as she. She'd only been through high school herself—I heard her tell Dad.

We raced down the walk to our starship, which was stationed at the front curb. After a minimum of preparation and strapping in, we went into cold-sleep; then the ship entered interstellar space. It took ten thousand years to reach Wineland, a planet inhabited by a tiny population of subhuman species.

Sarah Wineland was maybe thirty-five with silver-streaked brown hair. She smiled a lot and although she was a little overweight, the old-fashioned flowered dress she wore seemed to make that look right. She came out onto the big screened-in porch to let us in. She said, "Hello, Ann. Bob and Ellen have been waiting to play with you."

Hardly likely. "Hello," I whispered.

"Now you just take your time, Rose. Everything will be fine here."

Rose bent down and gave me a kiss on my cheek. A flowery scent whisked by me as she stood up again.

"Thanks, Sarah," she said. "It'll be around one o'clock. Bye now. Bye, Ann."

"Bye." I hoped she would change her mind at the last minute and take me with her, but of course she didn't. I was a worry and a bother—she wouldn't even tell me where she was going.

She clicked down the walk in her stilted shoes and climbed back into the starship. I watched as the ignition sounded, and then, all at once, the whole ship was enveloped in giant orange flames. The heat was so intense I had to step back, and tears fell down my face.

"She'll be back," Mrs. Wineland said, opening the door. "Don't cry—you're such a pretty little girl with those ringlets and big brown eyes. Don't spoil it by making a face."

I rubbed the tears away as we went into the house. Mrs. Wineland's livingroom was big and airy by any standards, but it had a strange odor. Furniture crowded the whole place—couches, endtables, coffee tables, hassocks, plant racks—every imaginable item was fitted in there. Bric-a-brac abounded at every turn, and I was surprised that the greater part of it had not been broken. Bob and his sister had a tendency to play with the stuff. Personally, I saw nothing fascinating about cheap gewgaws.

"The children will be right in," Mrs. Wineland said. "I think you all would like some Kool-Aid later. I'll mix some up."

As she went into the hall, Bob came past her into the room. He went immediately to a glazed statuette of a woman in an eighteenth-century dress of pink silk and ruffles.

"Hi," he said with finality. He fingered the hard curves of the flowing dress, but didn't look at me.

"Hi," I said. "Look, you don't have to play with me. I'll just amuse myself, and you and Ellen can—"

Ellen came into the room. She wore a white tee shirt like Bob, and green pants with patches on the knees. Fine yellow hair like her brother's clung damply to her forehead. She didn't smile.

"We have to play with you," Bob said. "Mom told us." In the month that I'd known him, I'd never seen him so sullen.

"Want to play hide and seek?" Ellen said with a kind of subdued hope. "We could go in the back yard."

I looked from her to him, then shuddered. The thought of crawling around in the yard hiding from these two was less than inviting.

Ellen caught the look on my face and frowned. "Well, what can we play?"

"Nothing," Bob said. "Nothing's good enough for *her*."

He turned and took Ellen by the arm. "Let's play hide and seek—you and me."

Ellen laughed. "Okay—out back."

They ran into the hall as if forgetting that I ever existed. Their shoes thudded against the bare floor and then the back door slammed. If I could have been all alone out there, I would have gone and played on the swing set.

I felt the glass growing around me until I was enclosed all around by a giant bubble. I floated over to the couch and bumped against the arm. The glass was one way—I could reach through, but nothing could get in. When I had eased the bubble onto the couch, Mrs. Wineland came in.

She sat down at the other end of the couch and smiled.

"The kids are out back—why don't you join them? You like the swings."

"I'll stay here for a while," I said. "It's cooler."

"But there's a breeze outside." Her voice was a little strained. I'd been to her house on three occasions, but this was the first time I noticed that she sat pressed up against the arm of the couch. I'd hoped she wouldn't be like everybody else, but now her eyes had that same look of secret horror. Even a smile couldn't hide the lines that crinkled her mouth the wrong way.

"I won't bother you," I said. "I'll just sit here and read a magazine." I reached under the glass endtable and pulled out a *McCall's*.

Mrs. Wineland tried another tack. "I'm going to clean, so you just take that out back and read it. Go on now."

She stood up to demonstrate her authority, then gave me a sharp look. So I had to play along—it was her house. But I knew she was afraid.

It had snowed in the back yard, and I climbed across the powdery drifts toward the swing set.

Dad sat straight and tall, cutting his steak up into little squares. On the times we had steak, he always did that—cut everything up at once, then ate very deliberately. He concentrated on the meat, hardly looking at me.

"This is tough, Rose." He glanced across the bowl of artificial daisies to Mom. "You pay four dollars a pound and it's not supposed to be tough."

"Maybe I cooked it too long," Rose said. Her eyes misted over a little and somehow I felt happy.

"Damn it, Rose. Four dollars a pound! I don't work ten hours a day for you to throw money away." He jabbed a piece of steak so violently that some peas fell off his plate onto the table cloth.

"You don't have to yell, Mark. I do the best I can—everybody makes mistakes."

"You're irresponsible!" For a moment Mark's face seemed ugly. Actually he's very handsome—the perfect combination of dark brown hair, and eyes shaded by perfectly-shaped brows.

Tears began to creep down Mom's face and her lips trembled. "I'm sorry."

Mark frowned and put down his fork. "No, I'm sorry. I don't know why I've been yelling so much lately. Money isn't that tight yet."

Rose looked at him and smiled. "We've been through a lot together all these years." She'd made him forget—it wasn't fair.

"But the meat's ruined," I said. "What about that? What about being irresponsible?" She had faked him out and he couldn't even see that.

Dad looked at me. They both looked at me, as if suddenly they were together and I was alone. And in their eyes was the same look of secret horror—even Dad. All at once I wasn't hungry any more.

I walked through the great hall, my billowy dress gleaming gold and silver. By the door was a narrow stone staircase which led round and round up to the top of the keep. I mounted each step sadly, thinking of my tapestried room and my dark, handsome prince, who would never come to put his arms around me. He belonged to Rose.

IMMIGRANT TO DESERT-WORLD

The heat alone wouldn't be so bad,
But the whole planet seems to come
In fire colors
(Sand in oranges and yellows of all kinds,
Lava in red and black,
And even the sky gas-blue),
One giant forge
Where the smithgod hammers out
Intricate iron-work intelligences.
At night, though,
When the starbeams strike the sand,
Muting and multiplying in reflections
What I see, I don't regret
What I called home.

—Ruth Berman

OMIT FLOWERS
by Dean McLaughlin

Dean McLaughlin's latest book is
Hawk among the Sparrows, *a collection
of his short SF stories. He lives
in Ann Arbor, Michigan, where he
owns his own bookstore, The Book Shop;
its SF section is, of course, superb.*

The doctor stepped out into the hall and closed the door. He paused, then crossed slowly to where the small group waited. He was tired; it was deep in the night, and nothing had done any good. The corridor was dimly lit except down at the end near the nurses' station. Quiet.

"I'm very sorry," he said. "Very sorry."

They took it well. It was no more than they had expected.

"And I'm sorry, also," he went on, still speaking slowly, for he was reluctant to speak the question his responsibilities required him now to ask, "that I must have a decision from you. But it is not a thing that can wait. I must know your wishes now."

He scanned their faces. The small young woman swallowed, nodded mutely. The heavy, older man looked stoic. "Of course," he said, his voice so hoarsely low it was almost inaudible. The older woman looked straight ahead through rimless glasses; what she saw, if anything, was hard to guess.

"The choice must be entirely yours," the doctor said. "But it must be made now. No internally sustained life-signs remain; even if we wanted to, the law would not permit us to keep the life support system connected. So: as you probably know, it would be possible to freeze him, in the hope that medical science of some future date might be able to revitalize him. It's a costly process, and the prospect uncertain, but it can be done."

He took a deep breath. "On the other hand," he went on, "as you may also know, certain parts of him are still in excellent condition. You'd get very good prices on the spare parts market."

He glanced down at his watch. "Which do you want? At most, we have five minutes before he starts to spoil."

LOUISVILLE SLUGGER
by Jack C. Haldeman II

The author of this strange little adventure describes himself as having patches on his jeans, gray in his beard, and sand between his toes. He was once crazy enough to put on a World Science Fiction Convention, but seems to have completely recovered now. (Your editor, who suffered the same lapse just 12 years earlier, knows exactly how he feels.) Mr. Haldeman—his friends call him Jay—has been writing more or less full time, picking up occasional very odd jobs along the way; for relaxation he fishes, stalks the marsh with camera, and shoots pool in the local honkytonk. Currently, he is working on an SF novel, Nightmare Station.

Slugger stood helplessly as he watched the ball arc over his head and clear the center field fence. Four to three—it was all over. He dropped his glove to the ground and started the long walk back to the dugout. The sell-out crowd was silent. He shook his head. They'd lost it; lost everything—the game, the series. Now those ugly Arcturians had won the right to eat all the humans.

It was a crying shame.

Too bad Lefty had sprained his ankle rounding first.

The UN delegates milled aimlessly around in their special box seats. They looked depressed and Slugger couldn't blame them. They were all overweight and would surely be among the first to go.

Well, he had gone the distance and that was the important thing. *How* you play the game is everything. Coach Weinraub always said that.

He hated going to the showers after losing a game. There was none of the joking around and towel snapping that followed a win. Maybe there would be a cold beer. That would be nice. He wondered absently who they *would* eat first.

The locker room was depressing—no beer at all, only warm Cokes and stale popcorn. He dressed quickly and slipped out the back door. The Arcturians were probably spraying each other with champagne.

He arrived at the Blarney a few minutes later. Usually he didn't go there, but tonight he wanted to go someplace where he wasn't known. He wasn't aware that his face was more widely known than the President's. He ordered a beer.

The bar was dirty and dark and the ruddy-faced bartender was the only one who could get a good look at his face. Luckily he was sympathetic and didn't let on that he recognized Slugger.

"Damn shame," said a man at the other end of the bar.

"Yeah, I wonder what Arcturians taste like. Do

48

you know anyone who's eaten one?"

"My brother-in-law's in the Forces, and he says they taste like corned beef."

"Yuck. I wouldn't eat one in a million years. They look worse than maggots."

"You ever seen an algae production plant? That burger you're eating was a slimy green plant a week ago."

"That's different."

Slugger played with the water spots on the counter in front of him as he listened to their conversation. He wished Lefty was around and they could joke things up, break some of the tension. Maybe he should give him a call. He'd said he was going home to his wife, but maybe he'd come out for a beer. Maybe his ankle still bothered him.

"I bet you wouldn't eat one of them."

"I'm not sure. After all, they were going to eat us and it seemed like the only thing for us to do. Anyway, we lost the game, so we don't have to eat them. Why worry about it?"

"Yeah, the game. Buncha clowns."

Slugger felt his collar getting tight. He gripped his beer glass harder to keep his temper down.

"The umpire should've been shot. I hope they roast him on a stick."

"It wasn't the umpire, it was the team. They looked like a buncha girls out there. Did you see that bonehead play old Mandella made? They shoulda traded him years ago."

"They gave him an error, didn't they? What do you want? He was two for five."

"Lousy singles with nobody on. He struck out in the fifth with the bases loaded."

"They had good pitching. Shut us out twice."

Slugger nodded to himself and ordered another beer. They did have good pitching. Have to hand it to them there. But hell, with six arms and twelve fingers on each hand, they *had* to have good control. A lot these bar-flies knew. They should have had to face those curve balls that dipped *just* right.

"You're all wet. We blew it—blew it real bad. Lefty only had one hit and he had to FALL DOWN! An easy double, maybe three bases and with Pedro batting clean-up, man, that would have been the ball game. But no, he had to go and trip over his own shoelaces. Couldn't even get back to first. What a clown."

Slugger had had enough. They couldn't talk about his friend like that. With calculated slowness, he stood up and turned to face the men at the end of the bar.

"It coulda happened to anyone. Wasn't his fault."

"Hey look, it's Slugger."

"Throw the bum out."

"Fantastic! Ten for seventeen in the series."

"Bet the fix was on."

"Can I have your autograph, Slugger? It's for my kid."

"Buncha sand-lot bums."

Slugger turned to the nearest man and grabbed him by the collar, lifting him off the bar stool.

"It could have happened to anyone," Slugger repeated. "A bad day, that's all."

He sat the struggling man down, missing the stool and dumping him on the dirty floor.

"But this was the last one, Slugger. We *had* to win this one."

"You win some, you lose some, and some get rained out," said Slugger as he walked to the door, stopping only to autograph a baseball someone held out for him.

Outside, the streets were filled with celebrating Arcturians. They were running around with knives and forks in their multiple hands. Some wore bibs with humorous sayings printed on them.

Slugger started the long walk back to his apartment. Many of the Arcturians he met congratulated him on his performance in the series. Others pinched his arms and buttocks. He felt like half a cow hanging in a butcher shop window.

It was growing dark and a cold drizzle had started. A young boy wearing a tattered baseball cap was standing on the corner, selling evening papers with the headline: HUNGRY FOR A WIN, THE AWKS COP THE BIG ONE.

The boy approached him.

"Say it isn't so, Slugger."

The great man just shook his head and crossed the street.

MINSTER WEST
by William E. Cochrane

In the beginning, Mr. Cochrane tells us,
there was high school and a three-room
collection of science-fiction magazines.
Later—1948—he was bitten by the
stagecraft/dramatics bug, something he's
never fully recovered from since. He's
worked at M-G-M Studios, NBC Studios,
and Douglas Aircraft; sold his first
story to John W. Campbell back in 1970;
and since then has alternated part-time
and full-time writing. His Hunt the
High Air *will be out soon from Berkley.*

Minster West was a business man, but he didn't like flying in the big transocean supersonics. He cherished the illusion that he was in complete control of everything he did, and the supersonic passenger service was too automated by far to make him happy.

For example: the plane was on the ground, at the Los Angeles Megaterminal, but the seat arms and safety belts wouldn't unlock to his boarding pass— simply because he had luggage. The luggage pod would have to be removed, unloaded, and sorted before his passcard would unlock the belts and let him deplane. All for his comfort, of course, but the delay was worrisome.

Minster West had been in Switzerland, to meet Albert North, a business colleague and a courier, carrying over two million Gold Certificate Dollars. Minster had met the courier, but not the two million. North had a neat little scheme which involved leaving the GCD's in Los Angeles and eliminating Minster West in Switzerland. As usual, Minster had been in complete control of that part of the plan and it had failed.

The worrisome part—the worry about the delay here at the L.A. Terminal—was because of Minster West's silent *bankers*. Their illegal ownership of the money was enforced by a violently rigid code. Loss of the money was failure; and failure meant death.

In Switzerland, Minster West had helped the courier to confess the location of the money, then had killed him—by the code.

Now, the problem was to get back to Bel Air and to Minster's patron—to talk long enough to convince him that the failure was the courier's, not Minster West's.

To do that, he had to get the money, have it available together with the proof that he had killed the courier. Anything less ... The delay was very dangerous ... Minster had no doubt that the loss of the money was already known. His patron would also know that he'd returned to Los Angeles. The supersonic flight from Switzerland made only one stop.

The aircraft door opened with mechanical clickings and hydraulic sliding sounds. The light bar on Minster's seat displayed PASSENGERS MAY DEPLANE in three languages.

Minster managed to be the first up the aisle, by crowding and moving firmly among the other passengers. He was the first to leave the plane and had the umbilical walkway all to himself as he let the slide-walk belt carry him slowly toward the terminal building.

Everything was under control.

Ten kilometers away, at the end of the tube-train line, was a parking lot for ground cars. In that lot were Albert North's vehicle and the two million Gold Certificate Dollars. In an inner section of his wallet, Minster West was carrying the ID cards, keys, and parking lot entry pass for that vehicle. He intended to board the public tram, pick up the courier's car, and drive it directly to the Bel Air address where he knew he would get a hearing. The senior *bankers* in Las Vegas were out of the question. They were inflexible. No. If he could get the money and his story to Bel Air, everything would be under control.

The umbilical tunnel opened into a glass-walled cubicle inside the main concourse. Minster felt the instant shock of exposure. Everybody could see him in this glass cage and there were only five other passengers behind him in the tunnel. He didn't want to be noticed—there might be people looking for him, even now. He had to get into the crowd in the concourse, get lost quietly.

He jabbed his boarding pass at the door lock. . . . And smashed against it. The door wouldn't open. He took his pass out, turned it over and put it back in the slot—several times—before he noticed the lighted panel over the lock:

UNAUTHORIZED EXIT
USE DOOR B
BAGGAGE CHECK OUT AREA

Minster West swore quietly and swung to the other door. One of the other passengers was already opening the door, glancing at Minster idly as he went through. The door shut quickly behind him.

Baggage . . . First it had held him in the plane and now the damn automated terminal wouldn't let him out until he picked up his baggage. The only exits that would work for his key-card would be the ones leading to the luggage off-loading area.

Angrily, Minster jabbed his card into the Door B slot and walked through. The door led, as he could plainly see through the glass walls, to an escalator running down to the lower travel-tunnels under the terminal. Down there he would presumably get other recorded, or visual, instructions to direct him to his luggage. Minster stamped angrily to the escalator. It was the only way out of the area and he didn't like being exposed to anyone who might be looking for him. Right now, the last thing he wanted was that useless luggage. But the quickest way out of the terminal was to pick it up and then get out to the ground car storage garage—fast.

Minster West saw the solitary man standing outside the glass barrier of the concourse. The man made sure that Minster saw him, moving over to stand directly opposite the descending escalator. He was motionless, in contrast to the hurrying crowd around him, and he was looking directly at Minster West, looking intently, as if to memorize him, and smiling slightly as Minster West dropped below the floor level.

Minster put a hand to the banister rail of the escalator to steady himself. He knew that face—the cold blue eyes, the one scar on the jaw line, the peculiar wide nose—Reagan Under.

Las Vegas was definitely out. Reagan Under worked for Las Vegas and his presence in the terminal meant he had a contract to recover the GCD's and kill Minster West. He wouldn't have been sent for a lesser job—to listen to excuses. Las Vegas had made their decision on that. Minster West was worth two million GCD's—dead.

"Now he *had* to get the courier's car to Bel Air. And he had to stay away from, or ahead of, Reagan Under as well.

Suddenly, the walls of the escalator were pressing in on him, closing him in a trap. The slow descent was intolerable. Minster began to walk down the steps, speeding the trip.

At the bottom was the rotating carousel of the terminal's transport system. Minster pushed his way through the turnstile, his boarding pass releasing one of the cars to him. On an impulse, he turned back into the turnstile alcove and spun the turnstile again, using Albert North's pass-card.

He didn't board the first car, but instead reached in to lock the safety bars back toward the seat and sent it moving out onto the travel-track. He boarded the second car and let the safety bars press him back into the padded seat. The car's linear motor drive had a top speed of only five kilometers per hour, but it was too conspicuous to walk down the service way beside the cars—he wanted to run—and the baggage drop was far enough from the deplaning area to make the ride necessary. The trick with the two cars was not a very bright one, but it was the best he could do. At least he had the immediate area to himself. He could see the heads of people in cars ahead of him, and there would be more behind him. But in the time he'd taken to reserve two cars and board the carrier, no one else had come into the carousel area. The traffic was light at this particular time and the illusion that he was alone in the crowded terminal was part of the design of the place. Travelers were made to feel that they were getting personal service, even from an automated airport.

Minster turned his head to see if any more passengers had boarded carriers behind him and caught a glimpse of the lean figure just getting into a car. *Under!*

How had he gotten into a transport tunnel for passengers only, when Minster couldn't get out? Well, Under was four cars behind. That would give Minster time to do something—get lost in the crowd. The baggage area was always full of people.

But would he get to the baggage area? Minster's back crawled at the thought of a high velocity pistol bullet. The back of the carrier was plastic, no barrier at all ... the four cars in between? Maybe they were blocking Under's fire. Maybe he didn't have a gun. It would be a risk, bringing a gun this close to the airport's locator police and the warning magnetrons at each boarding gate. No, that was foolish. Under would have a gun; a plastic, undetectable one, probably, but thoroughly lethal nevertheless. The question was, would he use it here ...

Minster looked frantically around the travel-tunnel. The brilliant tubelight panels made him feel exposed. He could be killed in here ... and the upholstered carrier-car would carry him along just as if he were alive—an upholstered, moving coffin, with Reagan Under following along behind.

No. Wait! The tunnel was as much a trap for him as it was for Minster. Reagan was too much of a pro to kill where he would be connected with the body.

"Attention! Attention!" The PA system echoed in the tunnel. "Please remain seated. Your carrier will come to a stop. This is an emergency message. Do not leave your carrier."

Minster sat forward. "What ... ?" He felt the carrier slowing. At the same time he saw thick plastic barriers sliding down from the ceiling. Metal plates were moving in to cover the track, and he felt the carrier settle to the surface of the track. He twisted his head. Was this a trap, arranged by Reagan Under? No. There was another heavy barrier dropping behind Minster's carrier. Also, he could see Reagan twisting his head in apparent surprise. He did not like the barricades either.

The PA system had repeated its warning and then

went on: "Nitrate sensors have detected the presence of an explosive device. The roof shields are for your protection. A bomb disposal squad will locate the device and rende—"

"*Whamm!!*"

The sound of the explosion was deafening in the tunnel. Even though the barriers blocked most of the sound, they did not remain unscathed. The explosive shock wave passed through their thickness, but where it reflected from the surface, the plastic cracked and crazed along inner stress lines.

Minster saw the barrier in front of him frost with shatter marks and felt pieces of its surface, blasted off by the shock wave, strike the carrier. At the same instant his ears stabbed in pain as the pressure went up, then dropped in a fraction of a second.

The bomb must have been close . . . in the car ahead . . . the one he'd called up for himself with his Minster West boarding pass. But how had a bomb been put on the carrier? *Under!* He must have been waiting by the carousel, must have planted the bomb while Minster was doing the trick with the courier's pass . . . or phoned down to have it done. It seemed impossible, but a bomb planted at random would have been useless, except to scare. And it had done that. A bomb that came so close to its victim was terrifying indeed.

Minster jumped, a nerve-jerk of fright bringing him upright in his seat as a door opened in the barricade, over near the wall. He relaxed almost immediately, relieved to recognize the uniform and armor of the Megaterminal's bomb squad. He could hear sounds again. His ears still ached.

"You all right, sir?" The rescueman pulled the safety bar forward. "Any injuries?"

Minster West shook his head. He didn't say anything. He was thinking over the next obvious question, trying to decide whether the automated computer could be tricked into helping him change identities, here in the tunnel. If the car ahead of him was supposed to be occupied by Minster West . . . and if the courier—Albert North—was rescued . . . Might trick somebody until the rescue squad discovered they didn't have a body.

"Come out this way, sir," the rescueman was saying. "You'll have to walk a short way, then we have some carriers moving forward of here. What's your name, sir?"

"Albert North," Minster replied, making his decision. "What happened? Was anybody hurt?" He made his voice sound alert, interested. He didn't want to lose any more time while some doctor checked him over for shock.

"Bomb exploded. In one of the carriers, looks like. Usually we get to them first. This way, Mr. North. Through this cubicle."

Minster had a glimpse of the track and the twisted, broken carrier; a sharp, tangy smell of the air which set him coughing; and then they were guiding him through the second compartment and into a third. This third compartment was open—the barrier had been pulled back into the ceiling—and a carrier was waiting with a rescueman aboard.

"Get in, sir," this rescueman said. "I'll be working the drive motors. Would you put your boarding pass on my log book, please."

Minster boarded the carrier, recorded his name, using the courier's pass, and pulled the safety bar back; all at the driver's instructions.

"Fine, here we go!" The driver worked a button on an open panel in the carrier's side. "Gotta work the motor on manual," he explained. "If we put the system back on auto all the carriers would move. And we got two-three barriers jammed down, back there. So I'm running a shuttle service. Take you down to Luggage Five and come back for the next guy. Works faster that way and everybody gets home, huh?"

"I'm for that," Minster said. "I'm going to pick up my bags and my car and get to a hotel for a drink—maybe two."

"Best plan in the world," the driver said, laughing. "Have you at Luggage Five in a minute. We can go a little faster on manual. Sit back and take it easy."

The luggage delivery area—Luggage Five—was filled with purposeful passengers. There was no indication that an explosion had occurred, anywhere.

Minster West reclaimed his false boarding pass from the driver, thanked him, and got out of the carrier. He put the pass in the entry slot at the baggage counter and read the number 516, displayed on the computer output screen. His luggage was inside that locker.

He felt the carrier pull away from behind him. The driver had probably waited to record the baggage number. That number, the computer memory-chip it would activate, and the boarding pass were enough to identify Minster West, or rather Albert North, and locate him. The rescue men didn't have to hold up passengers making out reports or asking questions. That could be done later.

Minster ignored the possibility that someone might try to trace Albert North. He didn't care. The only place Albert North could be found was in Switzerland, and he wouldn't be found for some weeks yet. His luggage, Albert North's luggage, was in Locker 516. Minster West didn't want the luggage—it was merely a disguising detail to let him blend with the crowd. What he did want was Albert North's ground car. He had to get to that ground car and deliver the two million to Bel Air. Quickly. In time to get Reagan Under called off his contract.

And to do that, he had to check out the luggage and leave this automated mousetrap—quickly. Every move he'd made so far had been directed by a computer, predictable. He was leaving a trail that Reagan Under could not only follow, but also figure ahead. Minster West was in no position to enjoy the time-saving, preplanned efficiency of the Los Angeles Megaterminal's system for handling the flow of passenger traffic. If he stayed a mobile statistic in the computer's program-flow he was apt to end up dead. And *that* wasn't one of the marvelous, modern services mentioned in the Terminal's brochures and press releases.

Minster got luggage locker 516 open, using Albert North's boarding pass. One travel case and a brief-case ... As Minster reached for the luggage, the ad-panel beside the locker caught his eye. Normally he ignored the low-sell ads in public buildings, but this one was for a rental agency—city licensed ground cars. *Drive Yourself*...

He edited his plans on the spot. The ride in an un-derground tube-tram was suddenly abhorrent. After the bomb in the tunnel he realized that the closed-in cabin of a subway tram would have him screaming in seconds. He could feel his nerves draw tight at the thought, a sick cold crawled his stomach.

Drive Yourself... He'd take a car out to the stor-age parking garage. That way, he'd be in the open, on the surface, and everything would be under con-trol.

The input peripheral on the ad-panel took Albert North's boarding pass and his credit card, showed a green panel and a service statement in a yellow panel:

LUGGAGE MAY BE DELIVERED
DIRECTLY TO YOUR
DRIVE YOURSELF VEHICLE
INPUT REQUIRED: LUGGAGE LOCKER NO.

And a pictogram showed him how to input the numbers.

Minster West followed the directions quickly and accurately. The locker closed and the luggage was on its way to his rental car. The ad-sign ejected a key-card: at once an ignition key, contract, and input card for the car company's billing computer. The bill-ing didn't bother Minster West. Albert North could pay it from whatever Hell he found himself in. The important part was the key and the car.

There was a good, comfortable crowd outside at the car stand. Minster was at home in crowds. He was skilled at standing in front of some people, behind others, moving sideways between people, at losing himself in a crowd. In seconds he was very hard to see.

The crowd was a fixed population, more people arriving from the terminal as the rental cars and shuttle busses took them away from the curbside. Minster was able to use them as cover without any difficulty at all.

His car finally rolled up on the automatic guide and began flashing its number. Minster slid out of the crowd and around the front of the car. He was inside and took possession with the key in one quick move. His hand was reaching out for the guidance control before the door had a chance to close. As soon as the CAR OCCUPIED light came on, he punched the FREEWAY—SOUTH button and then fastened his safety belt to cut in the drive. Minster was through with the automated air terminal. If he had his way he'd never enter another one. Minster was proud of what he called his free will. He fought to be able to control his own actions at all times. The times when he was forced to surrender his travels and his destinations to computer-operated escalators and people-carriers left him physically shaken. He felt he was surrendering some basic human dignity; worse, he felt like running in cold fear. Never again, Minster promised himself. He resolved never to place himself in such a helpless position again.

The rolling speed of the ground car was exhilarating after the terminal's moving mechanisms. The car took off with a squeal of tires as it detected an opening in the traffic flow, wove its way through the traffic control matrix of the Terminal's surface roads, following the guide lights and its on-board programming at maximum speed. Minster West gripped the seat arm-rests as the car leaned into the banked on-ramp and rose up the ramp toward the Freeway. The second stage drive cut in and the turbines whined up to the 35 kper approach speed.

Ah, this was the way to travel; free, fast.

This trip would be short. Minster coded the parking garage into the guidance panel. The car held to the Number One lane and to the off-ramp speed, swinging off the Freeway at the next down loop. A short trip. But at the garage Minster would check out Albert North's car and then he'd really take the Freeway route. Unhampered and uncontrolled; driving his own car—everything under control.

The rental car ran into a holding lobby at the garage. Minster unloaded the two bags, presented his claim-card and key to the ID plate of the garage's delivery system. Albert North had left the money in a black, Company two-seater. The travel bag and the briefcase went into the luggage deck alongside the two steel travel cases. Minster knew what was in those cases, but this lighted garage was no place to open them. There was most likely a random video system . . . Minster shut the rear deck and got in the car. FREEWAY—SOUTH was still the starting program, moving the car out of the garage and into the traffic pattern for the on-ramp.

At the top of that on-ramp, Minster checked the traffic coming up behind him in the faster lane, glanced at the car's avoidance radar, and noted that there was nothing in the red ring. Clear enough. He punched in the Bel Air code, then set the car's computer locator on the seven-digit address matrix of his Bel Air patron—the man he had to see, to talk to. His fingers moved over the input keys rapidly. The address had to be coded and accepted before the next off-ramp or Traffic Control would classify him as local traffic and vector him off the Freeway.

The car's screen displayed a route-map, showing the route the traffic computer had selected. Minster stabbed the ACCEPTED button and leaned back to enjoy the ride. The car swept over into the Number Two lane and accelerated slightly until the car ahead was in range of the red-zone radar sweep, then it slowed and went into station-keeping mode on that car, holding distance and cruising speed balanced in its on-board computer. This was fast enough for Minster West. The traffic would be light this time of day so the car wouldn't be slowed below cruising speed and start lane changing to maintain its matrix speed. Cruising speed would get him there fast enough. The Freeway from the Megaterminal swept up into the mountains, and swung left toward Los Angeles's center where Minster had programmed himself into a looping cross-over that went to the Bel Air residence enclave. It was a fast route; cruising speed would give plenty of time, but maybe a phone call . . . No. That wouldn't be wise. Minster West had the phone code for that ultra-anonymous Bel Air residence . . . But to call from a car . . . Unthinkable. The calls were radio broadcast to start—anyone could listen, and the police probably did; it was their kind of routine. And then, the Company cars were leased from a rental agency and their computer center controlled the traffic driving matrices. The center also relayed the car's phone calls, and recorded them. Minster West was confident of his ability to explain the two million and the courier. But an unsecured phone call would never be forgiven.

Minster West relaxed. He wouldn't call. He would be there quickly enough. He was out in the open air, in a car of his own; not subject to the electronic breakdowns and computer controls of public transport. He relaxed. Everything was under *his* control.

He looked around at the mountains and cloud-scattered sky. He liked driving his own car. The ability to go where he wanted to; the skill of matching decisions with the traffic computers when he picked a seldom used or off-frequency route; the adrenalin lift of moving at high speed in the midst of other cars, that were also running fast; all these made ground-car driving intensely exciting for Minster West, far more exciting than supersonic flight or rapid-transit tube trains. Minster liked to do things when he traveled. He hated to spend his time meekly handing his body over to a transport-terminal computer at one end of a trip and grab a travel-worn body back at the other end. Minster wanted more when he traveled. He didn't like being routed like a piece of luggage.

The supersonic flight and the tube transport were symbols of that terminal-to-terminal surrender, a passive trusting in machines and bubble-matrix memory programs to provide loving care and absolute safety in between stops. Minster hated public transport. He hated the abandonment of a part of his life—part of his control over his actions and movement—in exchange for a ticket or a boarding pass.

He growled to himself at the thought. He'd had to use that supersonic flight, but he wouldn't again for a long while.

§ § §

Somewhere he'd read that a business executive spends 65 percent of his life traveling in Public Transport Authority vehicles . . . probably in a PTA press release. Minster had no intention of wasting 65 percent of his life. He believed in being in complete control of his own life—of the traveling 65 percent too.

The car slowed, dropped down to tailgating speed and closed with the car in front, then slowed still further; maintained a legal separation from the car ahead while it flashed warning lights at Minster West and displayed a map panel on its output screen.

ATTENTION! ATTENTION!
CONGESTED TRAFFIC AHEAD
BYPASS ESTIMATED 15 KILOMETERS
DELAY IN TRANSIT 1.62 HRS
DRIVERS ON LOCAL CONTROL
DIVERT TO OFFRAMP-SURFACE

The map display was the car company's computer showing him an alternate route—two off-ramps away, and about the same ETA. The other choice was to sit out the congestion in bumper-to-bumper mode. No way! Minster couldn't afford the hour-and-a-half delay.

He quickly set up the acceptance code numbers displayed on the screen.

The car door slid open and a man got into the left-hand seat.

"Reagan Under!"

"The same, mister. I was going to blast you through the car windows, but you foolishly let your car stop . . ."

Minster looked at the dash. He hadn't indicated the bumper-to-bumper mode, so the car had come to a stop in order to hold its distance. It would start up again when the car ahead moved. In fact, it already had; they were rolling again.

". . . and I could get out and aboard. This way I get you and go back to my own car next time we stop. I put you in bumper-to-bumper mode and this mess tows you along while I get away. Simple, ain't it? Good-bye, Minster West."

"Hey, wait . . !" Minster was staring down the barrel of Reagan's gun—a silencer, a small revolver with a long barrel . . .

The car put out an audible howl and a HIGH SPEED LANE panel lit up. Warning lights were blinking violently, sonic signals stopping cars nearby, but Minster West didn't see these. The car went from a crawl to its near-max in a short eight seconds. The acceleration jammed West back into the seat padding. But more than that, the acceleration popped the foam speed-shells out of the seat and the dash. In two-tenths of a second, Minster West was cushioned and protected by the car's safety cocoon. He could see the

67

instruments and there was a cancel button on the seat arm to slow the car, but otherwise he was completely wrapped in the safety device.

The cancel button . . . He didn't have his hands on the seat arms. He hadn't been ready for the car to go into speedup—Reagan had surprised him—and the cocoon had folded his arms back against his stomach, trapping them there. He was hugging himself, comfortably, but unable to stop the car or to do anything about Reagan Under.

The car would go on to the end of its programming—the alternate route to Bel Air. But Reagan . . . Reagan would shoot, and Minster West would cease to worry about reaching the car's controls.

"Well, shoot," he called to Reagan. "Five minutes at Bel Air and I can explain everything. But I'm not going to sit in this seat all the way in and wait for you to work out some final death-time for me. Do it now, damn it!"

"Always gotta be in control, don't you." Reagan Under's voice was muffled by the safety cocoon. "Sorry, Minster. I can't oblige you right now. This foam-thing surprised me . . . jammed my gun hand. Feels like the barrel's stuck right in my stomach. Couldn't shoot you now, even if the gun was aimed right. There's a hunk of me in the way.

"So, we ride till your program cuts out. My car's locked right behind us. This doesn't change anything, just postpones it."

Minster saw the bumper-to-bumper car following along at the emergency speed. The rear-views showed it clearly. Reagan Under's car was empty, but controlling itself with the same electronic skill that Minster's car was exhibiting. In this speed lane the road/car feedback was surer than human reflexes; certainly safer, and the safety circuits overrode the manual controls—except for destination or slowdown instructions. Reagan's car should have been far back at this speed—in the green controller-zone. Reagan

Under must have gimmicked its electronics to get it to follow so close, so fast; but it would be available for his getaway, when Minster West's destination program finally steered them onto an off-ramp and dropped the speed.

In fact, the moment the car slowed enough to release the cocoons, Reagan Under would probably shoot. Minster West would have to do something before that time. What? Swerve the car? Reagan might miss once; not the second time.

Still, the control of the car would be a start—might help. His hand was folded up across his belly—his right hand—the holster of his belt-knife was a lump under his fingers. The plastic bodied, barely legal, belt-knife . . . He carried it just to defy the weapons detectors at travel terminals and hotels. He knew it was a weapon, but he'd never used it for a task more lethal than tough mutton, or an Australian cruise-ship steak.

Still . . . it could be used to carve away the foam, so he could get his hand on the arm-rest controls.

His fingers worked up the fabric of his jacket, snaked the knife out of the holster, then paused. He had the same problem that Reagan Under faced. Working by feel, he turned the knife, then tilted his hand so that the switchblade wouldn't snap open into his stomach. The blade came open, stuck against the plastic cocoon. Minster sucked in his stomach and felt the blade click into its lock. Good, now he had a knife.

A knife against Reagan Under's bullets. Not much, but it was a weapon and it put Minster in a frame of mind where he felt that he was in control of things again.

He started jabbing at the safety cocoon, the bits of plastic foam falling down on his hand as he widened a hole toward the arm-rest controls.

He held his eyes on the car's map screen, working the knife by feel, fascinated by the crawling pin-point of light on the map over-print, a light that marked his car's position and, by its visible movement on the map's scale, indicated the violent speed of the car. Ordinarily that light's motion on the map wasn't noticeable over any given minute—now Minster West could see it crawl. Lane Three speeds were in excess of 100 kpers and the car's turbine was screaming, the red overload panel flickering in and out as the car drove on the narrow edge of its safeties.

Minster worked frantically with his knife. The car would be through the mountains in minutes at this rate and the off-ramp to Bel Air was only ten-odd kilometers beyond. He had to be ready. An emergency stop just as the cocoons opened ... He *might* have a chance to use the knife.

The car swayed on its gyros. Minster's face and body pressed against the safety cocoon as the car swung into a swooping turn ... *the off-ramp!*

But not the one he'd programmed. Not yet! This was unscheduled! And cars don't run off the Freeway at max-speed. Off-ramp speeds are 30-35 kpers or less, which would open the safety cocoons—let Reagan Under shoot.

Any time now, the car would slow. It had to. Minster West gripped his knife more firmly, forgot his carving exercise, and set himself for a stab.

But the car wasn't slowing. It swept into a wide curve, leaving the Freeway. The g-forces of the turn jammed Minster West sideways into the cocoon, crushing the wind out of his chest and forcing his eyes away from the vision slot. One of his eyes, the right one, was forced completely closed by the pressure. He couldn't see the roadway, the instruments, the computer map-screen, or anything. Reagan ... If the cocoons freed Reagan Under, and he shot ... Minster West was helplessly off balance ...

The car held in the turn and nosed downward to drop below the Freeway level—Minster felt the sickening swoop in his stomach. Held the turn? ... So long, and at this speed, could only mean the off-ramp curved through 360 degrees. A full turn-around, or more. Where ... Minster West strained to move his head far enough to see the computer map. Where was he? Which off-ramp turned a full circle? He shoved as hard as he could, but his aching neck muscles could barely move his head. He gained an inch ...

The car slammed into emergency braking.

Minster heard the howl of the warning system as the brakes locked, heard two heavy bangs from the diverter vanes. *Panic brakes and reverse thrust!* A collision! The car was braking to keep from hitting something.

The deceleration threw Minster cruelly against the cocoon, driving his breath out in a great gasp. His eyes swam red, with shooting spots of yellow and violet; he could taste blood in his mouth. Then he rocked back against the seat, a release of pressure almost as violent as the braking. *The car had stopped.*

"YOU IN THE CAR!" The voice was gigantic, blasting into Minster's stunned brain. "FREEZE! THIS IS THE POLICE!"

Police. The money in the trunk ... The dead courier ... How could anybody have found out about the courier? Trans-oceanic telephones and satellite-bounce police computer-communications? His mind was working mushily, the shock of the turn and the stop had been severe, but he couldn't think of any way the courier's killing could have been discovered in so short a time. He'd been very thorough. Everything had been under control.

"STAY IN THE CAR! MAKE NO ATTEMPT TO GET OUT." The magnified voice continued, *"Your safety cocoons are being held in place by police over-rides. Do not attempt to leave the car.*

"The man in the passenger seat is under arrest. The charge is leaving a vehicle on the Freeway, unauthorized boarding of a moving vehicle, and possession of a firearm."

Reagan Under. They wanted Reagan Under. Minster allowed himself to feel triumph and satisfaction.

His head was clearing rapidly. And the fact that all his planning hadn't been in vain brought his optimistic spirit back. The police wanted Reagan Under. They didn't want him and they certainly did not want Albert North.

"When we move the cocoon away, toss the gun out the window. Then get out slowly. You are covered by computer-directed automatic weapons. If you make any unprogrammed motions you will be fired on."

Minster West was thinking furiously. The car was registered to Albert North. He'd checked it out of the storage garage using Albert North's keys and pass. The R & I computer would have told the police that long ago. What Minster was thinking about was if he should try to pass himself off as Albert North. He had all the courier's identification in his trick wallet . . .

No. That would be a losing game.

"You were observed and photographed by Aerial Two-Five. We know you are armed. Let's see that gun. Move!"

There was a soft hiss of hydraulics, and Minster's safety cocoon moved half-way back. Reagan Under began swearing.

Minster could see out the side window and a bit through the front, although he was careful not to move in order to look.

The car was inside a building. The off-ramp roadway ran right through it, except that the roadway was closed off by heavy steel doors at the end of the building. Heavy steel doors, a thick net webbing of some kind, and wide bumper barriers on the doors. The roadway was blocked and he could see a police riot tank—an armored car, multiple-gun turret and all.

"That's a good boy. Now come out. Slow! I want to see both hands—EMPTY!

"Mr. North, when the cocoon moves back, you stay put. Don't move; understand! You'll be all right. Just stay in the car."

Mr. North. They had ID'ed the car. Minster decided instantly that he would be Minster West. Albert North was on prolonged business in Switzerland. He'd ordered the car picked up . . . sent keys and passes . . . so he wouldn't have to pay two months' parking fee on the car. Keep the alibi simple and be stunned, thankful to be saved and it all happened so fast . . . Just be Minster West. He could be inconspicious, even in a crowd of police. Everything was under control.

"You're coming out nicely, Buddy. Keep moving!"

Minster sat unmoving as the police team swarmed in to search and 'cuff Reagan Under. He didn't even turn his head to watch. Disinterested and half conscious, Minster West was exercising his skill at fading into the scenery. His fingers moved covertly and the knife dropped back into its holster, where it was as normal as his belt or his pants. Enough citizens carried belt knives, so that even hyper-suspicious police wouldn't consider it a weapon.

Things were happening fast now. Reagan Under was being bustled into one of the armored cars. The turreted carriers were starting engines and backing away.

"Mr. North, are you all right?" A police officer was crouched beside Minster, his helmet pushed back and automatic rifle clanking against the car.

"Minster West. I'm not Albert North. He's still in Switzerland."

"Captain!" The patrolman opened the car door and stepped back. His manner was a shade less friendly and his hand hovered near the rifle as the officer came up.

Then Minster was stumbling through his story, parading his identification and denying any need for medical aid; all with the utmost sincerity. Believable sincerity, for the Captain was being polite and apologetic.

"You realize, of course, that once Traffic Control had photographed the violation, our crime procedures took over. The controller matrix locked your car into emergency override and brought you here, off the Freeway, where we could cope with the situation."

"Yes, yes. And thanks, of course. I don't know what I would have done . . . or what he wanted."

"Well, that's our business, now. We'll find out. The photographs alone are enough to get a conviction. You may be called on to provide a written statement, but other than that, you shouldn't be troubled.

"Now, we'll get you back on your way. Control Central has released your car controls, but my technician will be a few minutes reprogramming the memory bubbles in your on-board computer. When he finishes that, you'll be able to drive away. You all finished, Jack?"

"All done, Captain. She'll pick up Freeway Control now, sir. And your seat controls are reset. I tweaked up a couple of sloppy inter-junctions, too. She'll accelerate a little smoother." He grinned, glancing sidewise at his captain. "Drive a little faster in top blower, too."

"Ahh, yes," the Captain put in. "Well, watch your gauges on that, Mr. West. Don't want to get a speeding citation after all this, do you?"

Minster shook his head. He intended to dial minimum speeds all the rest of the way into Bel Air. "Can I go now?"

"Certainly. The roadway ahead of you will route you back onto the Los Angeles Throughway. Again, our apologies for placing you in an uncomfortable position." The Captain closed the door and stepped back.

Minster reached forward and entered the address code. He wanted to leave without appearing to hurry. The money in the car's trunk was nagging at his mind—too much money and too many police. He tapped the drive bar.

The car didn't move.

A VIOLATION light came on.

They had been toying with him. The police had no

intention of letting him go. Minster stiffened and looked at the Captain, forcing a puzzled expression to his face.

"Oh, sorry about that, Mr. West," the technician patrolman said, bending to pick up his citation recorder. "Once these violations go into the computer there's nothing anybody can do about them. This one got locked in along with the car-jacker's felony." He pushed the recorder's contact prongs into the fender slot on Minster's car and tore off the printout as it developed.

"Trouble, Sergeant?" the Captain asked.

"358-62K, Captain—Damaging a safety cocoon.

"You only have to get the repairs done and certified, ah, Mr. West. No big thing. Now, the car will move." the patrolman handed the citation printout in through the window.

Minster took the citation. He wasn't able to say anything. Instead he pressed the drive bar again.

The two policemen didn't think this final indignity called for comment either; they stepped back from the car.

POLICE CONTROL ZONE
MAINTAIN SLOW SPEED
FOR NEXT TWO KILOMETERS

The car's dash screen displayed the completely useless information and the car rolled forward out the door and along the roadway. Two kilometers brought Minster to the on-ramp and a spurt of acceleration took him swiftly up into the traffic. The car worked its way smoothly into the second lane, but Minster cancelled its programming at that point and held himself down to the cruising speed of Lane Two. He'd had enough high speed driving to last him for a good while.

The turbine whine, the vibrations from the road, the wind-shear noise, all served to calm and soothe Minster. Driving away from that police road-block had taken a toll on his nerves—if they had, at any moment, decided to search the car . . .

But they hadn't. Their own pictures and crime analysis programs had told them whom to arrest. Any other citizen was to be protected and released as soon as possible.

They hadn't searched.

Gradually Minster came to realize that he'd gotten away with it. He was out on the Freeway, the car back in his control again. The way he liked to be, alone, working out his own destination programs and punching his own driving codes.

Why, if this had happened on the public transport train to Los Angeles . . . trapped on the tube train . . . The police would have had to pull him off the train and would have opened and searched his luggage automatically—that would be the simplest way to get it out of the terminal. Some well-meaning, helpful policeman would have dumped his bags under the search-tubes without asking. The money in those metal cases wouldn't look like any possible combination of shirts and socks. Gold certificate bills were supposed to have small radioactive-ink tracers, and that many bills would probably trip an alarm. Minster shuddered as he thought what might have been.

But it hadn't—because he liked to do everything himself. It was precisely because he was a free agent, driving his own car, outside any mechanical control of the Public Transport Authority, that he'd been able to put over his bluff. A man who was independent enough to do his own driving still counted for something.

Minster sighed. He'd been breathing shallowly, caught by tension. This was a free, deep breath. The sky above him was clear; unusually clear. The heavy block and tower form of the Los Angeles megacity was beginning to take shape against the sky, over to the left. The sky might even be clear enough for him to see the gleam of the ocean when he got nearer. A really fine day.

Minster West folded his arms, and then, made uncomfortable by the memory of the way he'd been held by the safety cocoon, dropped them to rest on the seat arms.

He gave himself over to the pure enjoyment of his own personal power. This was the way he liked to live. On his own, doing a job because it had to be done, but on his own terms and traveling across the face of the land—up where he could see things—and select any destination he wanted. *A man ought to be able to direct his own life,* Minster thought. *That's what it means to be in control.*

Minster's thought was broken by the car's dashscreen flashing a message rectangle:

CONFIRM LEAVING FREEWAY
AT NEXT OFF-RAMP

and a position-map display.

Minster West leaned forward slightly and pushed in the CONFIRM button for the off-ramp for Bel Air. He'd be there in minutes, now. And no trouble with a PTA passenger terminal or any such fuss. He scanned the dash for all the normal-operation lights and grinned again.

Everything was under control.

IS PHYSICS FINISHED?
by Milton A. Rothman

Back in 1936, only a year after having helped found the Philadelphia Science Fiction Society, the writer of this scholarly article hosted the very first science fiction convention. In later years, he got his doctorate in physics at the University of Pennsylvania, was sole chairman of two World Science Fiction Conventions, worked at the Plasma Physics Laboratory of Princeton University, and wrote and sold SF stories and physics books. Dr. Rothman now teaches at Trenton State College and lives in Philadelphia.

One theme untapped in science fiction is the possibility of a future time featured by severe unemployment among scientists due to the fact that there is nothing left to discover. Already physicists are continually working themselves out of jobs, because as soon as a new development gets to a point where it is useful or practical, then it's no longer called physics, but becomes engineering, bio-medical technology, or whatever. And then the physicists have to run after something new.

What if someday there's nothing new left to discover?

While the screams of, "There's always something new . . ." or, "How do you know what new discoveries might lie ahead . . .?" die down, let me hasten to say that I am by no means suggesting that we are at or anywhere near the grand finale of scientific discovery.

However, some important developments of the past two years lead some scientists to think that we may be at least within sight of the end of the line.

KELLY FREAS

Let me make clear what I mean by this. I suggest the possibility that sometime in the future scientific knowledge will be essentially complete—so complete that there will be no way of adding more to our picture of how the universe works. We will know all the fundamental concepts and are laws of nature, how living and nonliving matter are put together, how it all operates.

I do not mean that we will know every fact in the universe. That is certainly an impossibility. Simply charting the location of every planet in the universe is a task that cannot be completed because there is no way of getting the data for planets billions of light-years away.

But mere listing of facts is not the aim of science. That's a job for almanacs and encyclopedias. A scientist looks for a description of the universe in terms of a model that allows him to understand how things work, allows him to predict how things are going to work, and allows him to put together devices that work according to his predictions. So what a scientist wants to know is: what are the basic building-blocks of the universe? What are the forces that hold these building-blocks together, and what are the laws that describe how these building-blocks operate to produce chemical reactions, biological systems, galactic systems, and so on?

To a scientist, a simple listing of the 100-odd elements is not that important, although it may be useful. What is important is the concept that all matter is composed of these elements, and most important is the idea that each element is made of a different kind of atom.

The notion of the atom as a basic, indivisible particle of matter originated with the Greeks, notably Democritus, but was resurrected by the English chemist John Dalton in 1803. It took many decades for people to get used to the idea that everything was made of these tiny, hard, unbreakable particles. And then, just as they were beginning to get comfortable with that idea, along came J. J. Thomson, who, in that miraculous final decade of the 19th century, showed that atoms were not, after all, the ultimate particles of matter, but that they had an inner structure—that there were smaller particles, such as electrons, to be found within the atoms.

From then on things were never quite the same. That climactic decade of the 19th century was the beginning of modern physics. Tools for probing into the center of the atom began to be developed, and during the decades that followed there was a steady progression of investigation pouring out new knowledge at a constantly increasing rate.

It was Ernest Rutherford who showed (in 1911) that you could investigate the structure of single atoms by bombarding them with alpha particles and seeing how these particles were scattered by the atoms. His results proved that atoms were like little planetary systems, with all the positive charge and most of the mass concentrated in the central nucleus, while the electrons occupied the space outside the nucleus.

That made a neat picture, and with it the theoreticians, using quantum theory, were able to explain a great deal about the behavior of atoms in the emission of light, the formation of molecules, and the like. However, the experimentalists wouldn't leave things alone. In 1932 James Chadwick learned that an entirely new kind of particle lurked within the nucleus. In addition to the positively charged protons there were neutrons—particles without electric charge just slightly heavier than the protons. The discovery of the neutron solved a mystery that had been puzzling physicists for several years: How it was that the nucleus of helium had four times the mass of a proton, but only twice as much charge. Now it was clear: There were two neutrons and two protons circulating within the nucleus of helium.

This meant that the nucleus was much more than just the hard, unbreakable core at the center of the atom. In the decades that followed the nucleus was found to have a complex structure of many parts, arranged in shells, quivering with jelly-like oscillations of many modes.

Furthermore—and as Alice would say, curiouser and curiouser—the protons and neutrons within the nucleus gradually became suspect themselves. It began to look as though they were not hard marbles either, but that there were things stirring and spinning around inside them.

Where would it all end?

Maybe it would never end. Maybe protons consisted of smaller particles, and these consisted of even smaller particles, and so on without end, like the proverbial fleas with smaller fleas.

Our own E. E. Smith suggested as much with the fourth, fifth, and sixth order particles he created in the Skylark stories. There was a nugget of truth in his association of fourth, fifth, and sixth order forces (or energies) with these subatomic particles, for physicists know from quantum theory that to create or observe smaller and smaller particles one must use greater and greater amounts of energy.

And so as physicists began to build bigger and bigger particle accelerators to reach into realms of higher and higher energy, they began to observe newer and stranger particles. First in reactions caused by cosmic rays and then in the products resulting from a barrage of high-energy particles colliding with atomic nuclei, these strange and baffling hordes of particles began to make their presence known.

There were the muons—particles that behaved just like electrons, except that they were about 210 times more massive than the electrons, and nobody knew why. There was a whole family of particles called mesons—pi mesons, K mesons, eta mesons—with masses greater than 280 electron masses, and with positive, negative, or neutral electric charges. Then, with even greater masses were a family of particles called *baryons* (the "heavy particles"), including the familiar proton and neutron, together with the lambdas, the sigmas, the cascade particles, the omega particles, and more—all with either positive, negative, or neutral electric charge.

How do you tell one particle from another? Simply by measuring all the properties of the particle. A particle, after all, is completely defined by a list of its various properties. An electron, for example, is a thing that has a mass of 9.1×10^{-31} kilograms, and a negative electric charge of 1.6×10^{-19} coulombs— and any particle that has these properties has to be an electron. Another important property is its spin— the quantity of angular momentum the particle possesses. The quantity of spin belonging to each electron is found to be 1/2 of an atomic "spin unit" in magnitude.

Spin plays an important role in classifying particles into families and in predicting how they behave. For example, the photon (the elementary particle of light) has a rest-mass of zero, has no electric charge, but has a spin of one unit. All of the "light particles" or *leptons*—the electrons, positrons, neutrinos, and muons—each have 1/2 unit of spin. The mesons, on the other hand, with various masses and electric charges, have zero spins. The baryons, including the proton and neutron, all have spins that are multiples of half a unit in magnitude—that is, 1/2 or 3/2 unit.

To complicate matters further, we keep in mind the fact that for each of the particles there is a corresponding antiparticle—a particle that is identical in every respect, except opposite in some essential feature of symmetry. For example, the positron is the antiparticle of the electron: it is exactly like an electron except that it has a positive electric charge instead of a negative charge. What about the neutron and the antineutron? The neutron has no electric charge, so you can't have the opposite charge, but it does have a spin, together with north and south magnetic poles, just like planet earth. The antineutron has its N and S poles reversed in relation to the direction of spin, so it can be distinguished in that way.

Accordingly, when you add up all of the ways in which particles can differ—counting all the different masses, electric charges, spins, and other more esoteric properties called strangeness, parity, and isotopic spin—you get a great many possible combinations. In fact, by the mid-1970's there were about five hundred different particles known. Nobody could believe that all of these hundreds of creatures were really "fundamental" particles.

While you could see the tracks that these things made in passing through bubble chambers and photographic emulsions, you could also see that these tracks were quite short, showing that these objects lasted only a very short time. In fact, the electron, proton, and the two kinds of neutrinos are the only stable particles. All the others are unstable and decay into particles with greater stability in times ranging down to 10^{-23} seconds.

Clearly, these things had to be merely clusters of other things that stuck together for a short time and then fell apart. The trouble was, nobody could see what kind of things were sticking together to create all of these scores of entities. The whole situation was an indescribable mess.

It was really too much to bear.

But after all, it had taken over 2000 years from the first notion of the atom to the clear understanding that atoms consist of electrons, protons, and neutrons. It only took another half century for the particle mess to proliferate beyond endurance. Then, in 1963, an attempt was made by Murray Gell-Mann and George Zweig, of the California Institute of Technology, to reduce the particle picture to a simpler one by introducing a new particle, the quark. In fact, they proposed three different kinds of quarks.

How, you may reasonably ask, do you reduce the number of particles by making up three new ones?

And why the funny name? Did they run out of letters in the Greek alphabet?

The second question is answered simply. Physicists tend to be whimsical creatures, and particle physicists are the most. At the time he made his proposal, Gell-Mann knew that he had a very wild conjecture on his hands and chose a line from James Joyce's *Finnegan's Wake* to provide a name for his new babies: "Three quarks for Muster Mark!"

The quark model brings order into the chaos of particles by a very simple procedure. Just assume that all of the particles heavier than the electron— the mesons and baryons—consist of combinations of a small number of quarks bound together. Then, by knowing the properties of each of these three kinds of quarks, you can predict the properties of all the known particles.

The whimsy of the physicist is again with us as he refers to these three kinds of quarks as three "flavors." The three quark flavors proposed in the original version of the theory are called u (up), d (down), and s (sideways or strange). Suppose we list just two of the quark properties that go with each of these flavors:

FLAVOR	SPIN	ELECTRIC CHARGE (Electron units)
u	1/2	+2/3
d	1/2	−1/3
s	1/2	−1/3

An electron has one unit of electric charge, by definition, which means that the u quark has a positive charge 2/3 the size of the charge on the electron. In the table above the s quark looks just like the d, but it does have a different mass, and also differs in this property called "strangeness."

In addition to these three quarks we must also have three antiquarks with the same spin, but with opposite electric charge:

FLAVOR	SPIN	ELECTRIC CHARGE
$\bar{u}$	1/2	−2/3
$\bar{d}$	1/2	+1/3
$\bar{s}$	1/2	+1/3

Now, how do we combine these quarks? There are just two simple rules. (1) All baryons are combinations of three quarks, antibaryons are made of three antiquarks, while each meson consists of a quark and an antiquark. (2) In combining the quark properties, spins may be either added or subtracted, while electric charges are added algebraically (taking the plus and minus signs into account).

A few examples show how this works. Suppose we put together two u's and a d to get a combination we call uud. We take the spin to be $1/2 + 1/2 - 1/2 = 1/2$. The electric charge is $2/3 + 2/3 - 1/3 = 1$. This gives us a positively charged particle with a spin of 1/2, which we recognize to be a proton. On the other hand, if we added the spins according to the formula $1/2 + 1/2 + 1/2 = 3/2$, we would have a particle with a single positive charge and a spin of 3/2. The particle that answers to this description is a baryon called the delta-plus.

Suppose, on the other hand, we combine a u and a $\bar{d}$. If we subtract the spins we get a combined spin of zero, while the electric charge is seen to be $2/3 + 1/3 = 1$. These are the properties of a meson of unit positive charge and zero spin, which we know as the pi meson (or pion).

For fun and games you can go through all the possible combinations of 2 and 3 quarks to deduce their properties. (Actually there are more properties such as strangeness, baryon number, and isotopic spin which we have not considered here. For more details see the articles on quarks and particles in the following issues of *Scientific American*: July, 1974; June, 1975; October, 1975; and November, 1976.)

Every possible combination of the three quarks according to the given rules produces a particle that is actually observed. And all the observed particles can be constructed according to these rules. This in itself is a most remarkable accomplishment. However, for about twelve years, every elementary particle physicist had to begin every lecture on quarks with the disclaimer that: "What we have here is a most interesting hypothesis that allows us to organize a lot of data, but the trouble is that nobody has ever seen a quark. The quark theory explains all the observed particles, but the quark itself is not observed."

And particle physicists are always wary of hypotheses made for the sole purpose of explaining an experimental result—the so-called *ad hoc* hypothesis. On the other hand, the neutrino hypothesis had been used to explain a lot of mysteries for many years before the neutrino itself was finally detected. So there was hope that the quark model represented something real in nature.

However, other—and serious—problems stood in the way. The fractional electric charge of the quark was exceedingly odd and took some getting used to. Whoever heard of a 1/3 electron charge? But then it was just a matter of getting used to a new idea that merely sounded strange. People had gotten so used to the idea that the charge on the electron was *the* unit charge, they had to revise their thinking drastically to get used to 1/3 or 2/3 of an electron charge. But there's no law of nature that says you can't have such charges.

This is the kind of creativity that makes scientific revolutions: to focus on an idea that everybody thinks is obviously true, and to show that it ain't necessarily so.

Another problem was more serious. There are three particles (known as the delta-minus, the delta-double-plus, and the omega-minus) which can only be described as ddd, uuu, and sss respectively—that is, combinations of three identical quarks. The trouble is that such an arrangement violates an exceedingly fundamental rule of quantum physics called the Pauli Exclusion Principle. This principle states that you can't have two or more identical particles of spin 1/2 within a single system. (For example, each of the electrons surrounding an atom must be different from all the other electrons in that atom in some way—in energy, angular momentum, or direction of spin.) This is such a fundamental principle, firmly embedded in both theory and experiment, that its violation would be a catastrophe to the foundations of physics. And according to this principle, a particle consisting of three identical quarks is impossible. But there they are.

The physicist always has a standard method of getting out of such a dilemma. If he can't explain the behavior of a particle by the old, familiar properties, he invents a new property. So in 1964 the suggestion was made by Oscar W. Greenberg, of the University of Maryland, that each flavor of quark carries with it a new property that comes in three forms or quantities. This new property is called "color" and there are three possible colors for each kind of quark. In other words, there are quarks of three flavors, and each flavor can have three colors, so there are nine different kinds of quarks altogether. (Don't take the word "color" literally. When we talk about a red quark, we are just using a term to describe an abstract property. We don't mean the quark is really red.)

Now add to this picture the rule that each of the three quarks put together to make a baryon has a different color—so the baryon itself is colorless (just as putting together light of the three primary colors gives white light). You now have a model that works. The big worry is still that nobody sees any quarks by themselves.

What we have, then, is a neat intellectual scheme for bringing some order into the chaos of elementary particles—a classification scheme, so to speak. But until 1974 there was no proof of the quark theory—not the kind of proof that would satisfy some of the hard-nosed skeptics in the business. As a result, while the theory became more and more sophisticated, nobody could be quite certain that this picture actually described something real in nature. Everybody was worried that the model was just a set of ad hoc hypotheses piled on top of each other, ready to collapse upon the discovery of one contrary piece of evidence, as did the ether theory of the 19th century.

On November 17, 1974, real physical evidence of a most unexpected nature finally came through. Experiments performed simultaneously at the Brookhaven National Laboratory and at the Stanford Linear Accelerator showed the existence of a new particle unlike any previously detected. Called the J particle at Brookhaven and the psi particle at Stanford, its mass was measured to be over three times greater than the proton mass. What excited everybody was the lifetime of this particle: even though 10^{-20} seconds is a short time, this lifetime was a thousand times greater than the lifetime of other particles of similar mass.

To give a vague idea of what this means: it was as though you shot a billiard ball into a triangular cluster of billiard balls—and then had to wait five minutes before the triangle started to break up. It was absolutely unprecedented.

The next year was a period of intense activity among theorists competing to make sense of these results, for everybody knew that this was Nobel-Prize-mining territory. Indeed, Burton Richter and Samuel C. C. Ting, the leaders of the two groups that discovered the new particles, did receive the Nobel Prize in physics for 1976. (The relatively short time between the discovery and the award is in itself quite unprecedented, and gives a clue as to the importance of these matters.) Every particle accelerator in the world capable of going above 3 GeV in energy hummed busily as experimenters searched for more jigsaw-puzzle pieces for the theorists to put together. Quickly the picture took form.

The properties of the new psi particle could be understood by considering it to be a new kind of meson—a combination of a quark and an antiquark. But in order to account for the large mass and long lifetime of the particle it was necessary to invent a new kind of quark—and naturally this new kind of quark had to have a new kind of property—a fourth flavor. This new property was called "charm"—another piece of whimsy. While the existence of charm had been guessed at previously for other reasons, the new particles really needed the presence of charm to explain why they behaved the way they did.

Accordingly, we think of the new psi particle as a combination of a charmed quark and an anti-charmed quark, labeled $c\bar{c}$. This combination was called charmonium, for it behaved somewhat like the positronium atom that had been known for some time—an atom consisting of an electron and a positron circulating around each other.

Most remarkable was the fact that starting from this model, the theorists could predict the existence of two new particles having greater masses than the psi, and what is more, they could calculate just what masses these new particles should have. The actual discovery of these additional particles was the most persuasive proof of the reality of the quark model. Physicists who had been skeptics for the past ten years became instant converts to belief in quarks.

It is hard to describe the excitement that churned through the world of particle physics during the years 1975-76, while the outside world was mostly unaware of what was going on. Each new discovery was transmitted within an hour by telephone to physicists all over the world. There was no waiting for publication in journals. Those in the field gradually awoke to the fact that they were living through the most extraordinary revolution in science since those days of 1895 when modern physics began—when the discovery of X-rays, radioactivity, the electron, the photoelectric effect were the first tiny steps in the development of elementary particle physics.

Now, after 80 years of the most intense effort, it began to appear as though scientists were on the verge of understanding something really fundamental about the structure of matter.

This basic understanding can be boiled down to a few elegantly simple ideas:

1. Everything is made of a small number of particles (and antiparticles).
2. These particles interact by means of a very small number of forces, probably no more than four.
3. These forces arise as the result of a constant interchange of force-carrying particles (quanta) continually going back and forth between the fundamental particles.

The working out of these basic principles is quite complicated, and is the subject of the branch of physics known as quantum field theory. This most esoteric branch of physics deals with the way particles attract and repel, join together, fragment each other, create new particles, and engage in all possible activities under the urgings of the fundamental forces.

In quantum field theory we don't just accept the explanation given in freshman physics that an electron attracts a proton because there is an "electric field" between them that somehow carries the force through space. Instead, we carry the explanation down to a lower level of abstraction by saying that the electric field arises as a result of a continual interchange of photons traveling back and forth between the electron and proton. The photon is the quantum of electromagnetic energy whose activity creates the effect of an electric field.

As we have seen, the number of fundamental particles is rather small, once we accept the quark model. There are to begin with the four light particles (the leptons). These are the electron, the electron-neutrino, the muon, and the muon-neutrino.

(There are two kinds of neutrinos because some neutrinos only associate with electrons, and others only associate with muons.) Then there are the four flavors of quarks, the up, down, strange, and charmed—with three colors for each flavor.

Interestingly enough, all normal matter is made up of only four of these eight particles: the electron, the electron-neutrino, the up quark, and the down quark. The others only show up in reactions formed in high-energy accelerators. Nobody knows why they exist.

The most interesting feature of all this is that these particles do not appear to have any size at all; they behave just like mathematical points. The size of neutrons, protons, and other such particles is entirely due to the spaces between the quarks that make them up.

If this is so, then we have reason to think that we have reached the end of the line as far as particles are concerned. It is hard to see how a mathematical point can be constructed out of anything smaller. This is the reason for some of the excitement going on today—the possibility that maybe—just *maybe*—we know what the most fundamental particles really are. (More different kinds of quarks might yet be found, but that's another story.)

As for the basic forces that control the actions of all the particles, the number of these forces is not quite certain, but is probably no greater than four. Maybe it is three or two. Lots of people—beginning with Einstein—would like to have only one fundamental force. That is, they would like to be able to reduce all that happens in nature—from the subnuclear to the astronomical—down to the operation of a single kind of force.

So far nobody has been able to do this, but some interesting progress in that direction has taken place. To begin with, it has been apparent for the past few decades that everything happening in nature is controlled by no more than four fundamental forces: gravitational, electromagnetic, and two types of nuclear forces.

All of the things that happen on an astronomical scale—interactions between planets, stars, galaxies—are controlled by the gravitational force (with the exception of such things as the emission of light and the production of magnetic fields). This force is an attraction between all objects, and to a first approximation is described by Newton's law of gravitation. However, when you start dealing with things on a very large scale—bigger than a star— then you must use the more accurate description of gravitation given by Einstein's general theory of relativity. In terms of quantum field theory, the gravitational force arises from an interchange of particles called gravitons (each with a spin of 2 units) between the objects attracting each other.

A most important feature of gravitation is the fact that there is only one kind of mass, and therefore only one kind of gravitational force—which happens to be an attraction. (And it's a good thing, too.)

All of the activities taking place on an atomic level—and this includes things such as the structure of molecules, chemical reactions, the workings of transistors, adhesion, friction, the emission of light, etc., etc.—are governed by the electromagnetic force. This most familiar of all the forces is quite a strong one. Within an atom the electromagnetic force is some 10^{35} times stronger than the gravitational force, which explains why we don't pay any attention to gravity when dealing with things smaller than a breadbox.

Since the electromagnetic interaction arises from two kinds of charges (positive and negative), we find that there are two kinds of electrical forces— repulsions as well as attractions. It is this feature that makes it possible for us to handle the EM force and do all kinds of useful things with it.

There are two kinds of forces that make themselves felt when two particles come very, very close together. These are the strong nuclear force and the weak nuclear force. The strong nuclear force is the one that holds neutrons and protons together inside the atomic nucleus. With the new quark model we can describe the nuclear force as the summing up of all the forces between the six quarks that make up the neutron and proton being pulled together. This interquark force, according to quantum field theory, arises as a result of the exchange of quanta between the quarks. These quanta have been given the name of *gluons*, because they supply the nuclear glue that holds the core of the atom together.

Here the theory begins to get complicated, because it requires eight different kinds of gluons (different color combinations) to account for the interactions between different colored quarks. The theory of the interquark force is just on the edge of barely-understood contemporary physics—in fact, there are several competing theories vying for acceptance. All of these theories try for a solution to one great mystery still outstanding: why don't we ever see individual quarks with their fractional electric charges?

There are a number of possible explanations, but the one that seems to be in favor is the idea that the force between quarks is of a kind that we have never seen before. You know that the force between two electric charges gets weaker as the charges move farther away from each other. As a result, you can separate an electron from a proton with a definite amount of energy.

In contrast, the force between two quarks is supposed to stay constant in magnitude as the two quarks are separated from each other. The result is that when you try to pull two quarks apart you must put in an enormous amount of energy. So much energy is required, in fact, that it is enough to create a pair of new particles: a quark and an antiquark. (This process has been known for a long time. Whenever enough energy is available, a particle-antiparticle pair is produced.) These new quarks immediately join onto the original quarks you tried to separate.

Suppose, for example, that you started by trying to break a meson into a quark and an antiquark. In doing so you create another quark and antiquark. Each quark couples to an antiquark, and you end up with two mesons. So you never have a chance to see the separated quarks.

You see that we have here an unusual situation. We have a theory that depends on the existence of quarks. And yet quarks are never observed. We sneak our way out by explaining why the free quarks are never observed.

You might object that this is just a sleight of hand trick and that you can make up any kind of theory you want in this manner. (It's like the joke about the man who keeps tigers away by snapping his fingers. Snapping the fingers must really work, because you don't see any tigers around, do you?) The point is that the theory explains a great many other things which are observed—so it must stand on its ability to give a consistent picture of everything we see happening.

The fourth force—the weak nuclear force—plays a role in certain nuclear reactions such as beta decay, the emission of electrons from radioactive nuclei. It is a subtle force and the reasons for its existence have not been clear. However, some recent work, both experimental and theoretical, leads people to believe that the weak force is not a separate and distinct force, but that the weak force and the electromagnetic force are two aspects of a single fundamental force. This reduces the four forces to three. There is an effort to show that the strong force is also related to the weak and the electromagnetic. That would leave the gravitational force standing alone. Someday that may be joined to the other three, leaving us with the unified field theory that Einstein spent most of his life seeking.

This short description gives just the barest sketch

of the ideas that have been proposed by particle physicists during recent years. This is a part of physics where imagination plays as great a role as it does in writing science fiction. In fact, a lot of people thought the quark theory was science fiction for a long time.

Now we can ask ourselves what all of these new discoveries have to do with the writing of science fiction. For some writers, of course, there is very little connection. To them science fiction is pure fantasy, and the scientific background is just a setting for high adventure. To other authors the science is taken more or less seriously, but with the attitude that nothing is known for sure, so that new discoveries made in the future may well overturn everything we now know.

However, I would take the point of view that at least *some* of the principles of physics have been proven so thoroughly that there is very little likelihood of their being overthrown. The big problem is to decide what parts of physics are permanent and which parts are still subject to change. It would take an entire book to go into this question, and in fact I wrote such a book a few years ago. (*Discovering the Natural Laws: The Experimental Basis of Physics*, Doubleday, 1972.)

For now, let us ask the question: What will happen if the ideas described in this article turn out to be true? What does this knowledge of particles and forces do to some of the conventions of science fiction?

Take the gravitational force, for example. Everything known about this force tells us that all objects attract each other. There is no gravitational repulsion. (Remember, that's because there is only one kind of mass, as opposed to two kinds of electric charge.) This means that there is no way of arranging things so that they do anything besides attract each other. There's no way of arranging matter into an antigravity device or a gravity shield.

You see how understanding the properties of elementary particles allows you to make important statements about human-size objects. This is the fundamental reason why it is important to spend hundreds of millions of dollars on elementary particle research.

Often, however, this game gets us into great controversy. This is because when we say that all things are made up of a few kinds of particles, subject to the action of a few different kinds of forces, it's important to realize that we mean *all things*. And this includes living organisms.

Now there are a lot of people who object to this kind of argument, which they call *reductionism*. Reductionism means that the actions of biological systems can be reduced to the laws of physics and chemistry. I suspect that the basic reason for the objections to this notion are emotional and religious. It goes against the grain of many people to think that there's nothing more to man and woman than electrons and quarks and photons. Actually there is more to an animate being than a random collection of particles; there is a marvelous *organization* of matter into a creature that has self-awareness.

The fundamental question is: can this consciousness be explained without the use of some kind of *élan vital* or psychic force? I have seen serious papers in physics journals attempting to prove that single atoms and molecules have consciousness. (At least I think they were serious; they seemed too elaborate to be part of a joke.)

It is important that questions like this be settled. For if the four forces of the physicist are all the forces there are, then we can make some definite statements about the various forms of psi phenomena that we deal with in science fiction. Any of the various manifestations of psi such as telepathy or teleportation or poltergeist effects must be the result of some kind of physical force going through space from a transmitter to a receiver. What do we know about our four forces, and what do they tell us about psi?

We know that gravitation is much too weak to account for any psi phenomena. As for the nuclear forces and interquark forces, they only act over very short distances (less than 10^{-13} cm), so they can't account for any kind of signal going from one brain to another. This leaves the electromagnetic interaction as the only long-range force with sufficient strength to carry detectable signals or to move things around.

But if you put numbers into the equations and ask how a human brain can project enough energy to accomplish anything important at large distances, then you run into trouble. Measurements of electromagnetic fields around the brain show that a few centimeters from the skull they are so weak as to be barely detectable with the most sensitive instruments available. In fact, these measurements must be made within a shielded room—otherwise the signals would be buried in the noise of the stray electromagnetic fields that are present continuously, originating in house wiring, distant lightning flashes, etc.

In other words, the electromagnetic force is the only force available to explain telepathy, but the explanation is most difficult for me to believe. As for teleportation or poltergeists, there is simply no way for the brain to concentrate enough energy and project it through space to move a material object, bend a spoon, or bang on walls. For me to believe in any of these, I'd have to tear up my physicist's union card.

Whenever we get into a discussion of science in science fiction, there is no way of avoiding the fiercely controversial issue of faster-than-light travel. Our knowledge of fundamental particles shows no way to do this trick. If all matter is made of the particles we have been describing, and if they interact by means of the four fundamental forces, then any machine we make to propel a space ship must consist of the same kind of particles and the only kind of forces it has to work with are these same four forces.

Now all of these particles and all of these forces

behave in accordance with Einstein's principle of relativity. This is not just a matter of theory, but is a fact that has been verified to a very high degree of accuracy by hundreds of different kinds of experiments. No phenomenon in nature has ever been observed that is in conflict with the principle of relativity.

As every reader of science fiction must know by now, one of the foundation-stones of relativity is the rule that no object, energy, or signal can travel faster than the speed of light in a vacuum. While particles called tachyons have been proposed which are supposed to go faster than light (but never slower), these are not particles of ordinary matter. Even if they exist they could not help you go faster than light, because the particles of your own body must still behave according to the regular laws. On top of that, tachyons have never been observed and no effects due to tachyons have ever been observed, so the entire proposal remains an unverified hypothesis that was good fun and games while it lasted, but need not be taken seriously.

The tachyon hypothesis was a little bit of science fiction. It tried to point out something that *might be* true. That's the job of science fiction. Science, on the other hand, tries to pick out what *is* among all the *might be's*. Sometimes science opens new doors, outpacing science fiction in discovery. See how space has turned out to be more complex than science fiction ever imagined, the vacuum between the stars being filled with streams of plasma, while strange objects such as quasars, pulsars, neutron stars, and black holes inhabit the void.

On the other hand, science can close us in with walls of reality. The moment we got close-up photographs of Mars, science fiction writers could no longer write stories about the Martian canals. The first real information about the atmosphere of Venus killed every prospective story about the jungles of the cloudy planet.

It's easy to accept first-hand information like that. It's not so easy to accept the more indirect and abstract facts about relativity. For that reason I'm sure that science fiction writers are going to continue to use faster-than-light-travel as the road to other worlds.

As for the notion that we now know what the truly fundamental particles are, there is no agreement about this among physicists. The quark theory has raised as many questions as it has settled. How many quarks are there? Are quarks really fundamental, or is there another level below? Can all the forces be unified?

Furthermore, there are some serious questions at the very foundations of quantum theory which have been lying about unanswered for the past fifty years. There is an underground movement among physicists trying to bring these questions out into the open. Einstein and Bohr fought over these questions during the 1920's and 30's, and many people feel that the issues have never been really settled, but have simply been shoved under the rug.

It appears, then, that the foundations of physics are in a healthy state of turmoil, and that there is no danger that smart, thoughtful scientists are going to run out of problems to solve. At least, not for a few years.

GOOD TASTE
by Isaac Asimov

*The author was born in Russia, moved to
Brooklyn when he was three (with some
help from his parents), lived for many
years in Boston, and now lives in New
York City with his charming wife, Janet.*

KELLY FREAS

It was quite clear that it would not have happened—the family would not have been disgraced and the world of Gammer would not have been stunned and horrified—if Chawker Minor had not made the Grand Tour.

It wasn't exactly illegal to make the Grand Tour but, on Gammer at least, it was not really socially acceptable. Elder Chawker had been against it from the start, to do him justice, but then Lady Chawker took the side of her minor and mothers are, at times, not to be withstood. Chawker was her second child (both of them sons, as it happened) and she would have no more, of course, so it was not surprising that she doted on him.

Her younger son had wanted to see the Other-Worlds of the Orbit and had promised to stay away no longer than a year. She had wept and worried and gone into a tragic decline and then, finally, had dried her eyes and spoken stiffly to Elder Chawker—and Chawker Minor had gone.

Now he was back, one year to the day (he was always a young man to keep his word, and besides which the Elder's support would have ceased the day after, never fear) and the family made holiday.

Elder wore a new black glossy shirt but would not permit the prim lines of his face to relax, nor would he stoop to ask for details. He had no interest—no interest *whatever*—in the Other-Worlds with their strange ways and with their primitive browsing (no better than the ways on Earth of which Gammer-people *never* spoke). He said, "Your complexion is dirtied and spoiled, Chawker Minor." (The use of the full name showed his displeasure.)

Chawker laughed and the clear skin of his rather thin face crinkled. "I stayed out of the sun as much as I could, Elder-mine, but the Other-Worlders would not always have it so."

Lady Chawker would have none of that either. She said warmly, "It isn't dirtied at all, Elder. It breathes a warmth."

"Of the Sun," grumbled Elder, "and it would be next that he would be grubbing in the filth they have there."

"No farming for me, Elder. That's hard work. I visited the fungus vats at times, though."

Chawker Major, older than Minor by three years, wider of face, heavier of body, but otherwise of close resemblance, was torn between envy at his younger brother's having seen different worlds of the Orbit and revulsion at the thought of it. He said, "Did you eat their Prime, Minor?"

"I had to eat something," said Chawker Minor. "Of course, there were your packages, Lady-mine. Life-savers, sometimes."

"I suppose," said Elder Chawker with distaste, "the Prime was inedible there. Who can tell the filth that found its way into it."

"Come now, Elder-mine." Chawker paused, as though attempting to choose words, then shrugged. "Well, it held body and soul together. One got used to it. I won't say more than that. —But Elder-Lady-mine, I am so glad to be home. The lights are so warm and gentle."

"You've enough of the Sun, I take it," said Elder. "But you *would* go. Well, welcome back to the inner world with light and warmth under our control locked away from the patch and blaze of sunshine. Welcome back to the womb of the people, as the saying goes."

"Yet I'm glad I went," said Chawker Minor. "Eight different worlds, you know. It gives you a view you don't have otherwise."

"And would be better off not having," said Elder.

"I'm not sure about that," said Chawker Minor, and his right upper eyelid trembled just slightly as he looked at Major. Chawker Major's lips compressed but he said nothing.

§ § §

It was a feast. Anyone would have had to admit that, and in the end it was Chawker Minor himself, first to push away. He had no choice; Lady would else have kept on supplying him with samples out of what seemed to be a bottomless larder.

"Lady-mine," he said, affectionately, "my tongue wearies. I can no longer taste anything."

"*You* not taste?" said Lady. "What kind of nithling-story is that? You have the skill of the Grand-Elder himself. At the age of six, you were already a Gustator; we had endless proofs of that. There was not an additive you could not detect even when you could not pronounce them right."

"Taste-buds blunt when not used," said Elder Chawker, darkly, "and jogging the Other-Worlds can utterly spoil a man."

"Yes? Well, let us see," said Lady. "Minor-mine, tell your doubting Elder what you have eaten."

"In order?" said Chawker Minor.

"Yes. Show him you remember."

Chawker Minor closed his eyes. "It's scarcely a fair test," he said. "I so relished the taste I did not pause to analyze it; and it's been so long."

"He has excuses. See, Lady?" said Elder.

"But I will try," Chawker Minor said hastily. "In the first place, the Prime base for all of them is from the fungus vats of the East Section and the 13th corridor within it, I believe, unless great changes have been made in my absence."

"No, you are right," said Lady, with satisfaction.

"And it was expensive," said Elder.

"The prodigal returns," said Chawker Major, just a bit acidly, "and we must have the fatted fungus, as the saying goes. —Get the additives, Minor, if you can."

"Well," said Chawker Minor, "the first dab was strongly Spring Morning with added Leaves A-Freshened, and a touch, not more than a touch, of Spara-Sprig."

"Perfectly right," said Lady, smiling happily.

Chawker Minor went on with the list, his eyes still closed, his taste-memory rolling backward and forward luxuriously over the tang and consistency of the samplings. He skipped the eighth and came back to it.

"That one," he said, "puzzles me."

Chawker Major grinned. "Didn't you get any of it?"

"Of course I did. I got most of it. There was Frisking Lamb—not Leaping Lamb, either, Frisking, even though it leaned just a little toward Leaping."

"Come on, don't try to make it hard. That's easy," said Chawker Major. "What else?"

"Green-Mint, with just a touch of Sour-Mint— both—and a dusting of Sparkle-Blood. —But there was something else I couldn't identify."

"Was it good?" asked Chawker Major.

"Good? This isn't the day to ask me that. Everything is good. Everything is succulent. And what I can't identify seems very succulent. It's close to Hedge-Bloom, but better."

"Better?" said Chawker Major, delightedly. "It's mine!"

"What do you mean yours?" said Chawker Minor.

Elder said, with stiff approval, "My stay-at-home son has done well while you were gone. He devised a computer-program that has designed and produced three new life-compatible flavor-molecules of considerable promise. Grand-Elder Tomasz himself has given one of Major's constructions tongue-room, the very one you just tested, Flyaway-Minor-mine, and has given it his approval."

Chawker Major said, "He didn't actually say anything, Elder-mine."

Lady said, "His expression needed no words."

"It *is* good," said Chawker Minor, rather dashed at having the play taken away from him. "Will you be entering for the Awards?"

"It has been in my mind," said Chawker Major, with an attempt at indifference. "Not with this one—I call it Purple-Light, by the way—but I believe I will have something clse, more worthy of the competition."

Chawker Minor frowned. "I had thought that—"

"Yes?"

"—that I am ready to stretch out and think of nothing. Come, half a dab more of Major's construction, Lady-mine, and let's see what I can deduce concerning the chemical structure of his Purple-Light."

§ § §

For a week, the holiday atmosphere in the Chawker household continued. Elder Chawker was well known in Gammer and it seemed that half the inhabitants of the world must have passed through his Section before all had had their curiosity sated and could see with their own eyes that Chawker Minor had returned unscathed. Most remarked on his complexion, and more than one young woman asked if she might touch his cheek, as though the light tan were a layer that could be felt.

Chawker Minor allowed the touch with lordly complacence, though Lady disapproved of these forward requests and said so.

Grand-Elder Tomasz himself came down from his aerie, as plump as a Gammerman ever permits himself to be and with no sign that age or white hair had blunted his talents. He was a Master-Gustator such as Gammer might never have seen before despite the tales of Grand-Elder Faron of half a century ago. There was nothing that Tomasz tongued that did not open itself in detail to him.

Chawker Minor, who had no great tendency to underrate his own talent, felt no shame in admitting that what he himself had, innately, could not yet come anywhere near the old man's weight of experience.

The Grand Elder who, for nearly twenty years now, had governed the annual Awards festival by force of his skill, asked closely after the Other-Worlds which, of course, he himself had never visited.

He was indulgent, though, and smiled at Lady Chawker. "No need to fret, Lady," he said. "Young people these days are curious. In my time we were content to attend to our own cylinder of worth, as the saying goes, but these are new times and many are making what they call the Grand Tour. Good, perhaps. To see the Other-Worlds—frivolous, Sun-drenched, browsive, non-gustational, without a taste-bud to content themselves with—makes one appreciate the eldest brother, as the saying goes."

Grand-Elder Tomasz was the only Gammerman whom Chawker Minor had ever heard actually speak of Gammer as "the eldest brother" although you could find it often enough in the video-cassettes. It had been the third colony to be founded in the Moon's orbit back in the pioneering years of the twenty-first century; but the first two, Alfer and Bayter, had never become ecologically viable. Gammer had.

Chawker Minor said, with tactful caution, "The Other-World people never tired of telling me how much the experience of Gammer meant to all the worlds that were founded afterward. All had learned, they said, from Gammer."

Tomasz beamed. "Certainly. Certainly. Well said."

Chawker Minor said, with even greater caution, "And yet such is self-love, you understand, Grand-Elder, that a few thought they had improved on Gammer."

Grand-Elder Tomasz puffed his breath out through his nose (never breathe through your mouth any more than you can help, he would say over and over again, for that blunts the Gustator's tongue) and fixed Chawker with his deep blue eyes that looked the bluer for the snow-white eyebrows that curved above them.

"Improved in what way? Did they suggest a specific improvement?"

Chawker minor, skating over the thin ice and aware of Elder Chawker's awful frown, said softly, "In matters that they value, I gather. I am not a proper judge of such things, perhaps."

"In matters that *they* value. Did you find a world that knows more about food chemistry than we do?"

"No! Certainly not, Grand-Elder. None concern themselves with that, as far as I could see. They all rely on our findings. They admit it openly."

Grand-Elder Tomasz grunted. "They can rely on us to know the effects and side-effects of a hundred thousand molecules, and each year to study, define and analyze the effects of a thousand more. They rely on us to work out the dietary needs of elements and vitamins to the last syllable. Most of all, they rely on us to work out the art of taste to the final, most subtly convoluted touch. They do so, do they not?"

"They admit all this, without hesitation."

"And where do you find computers more reliable and more complex than ours?"

"As far as our field is concerned, nowhere."

"And what Prime did they serve?" With heavy humor, he added, "Or did they expect a young Gammerman to browse."

"No, Grand-Elder, they had Prime. On all the

worlds I visited they had Prime; and on all those I did not visit, I was told, there was also Prime. Even on the world where Prime was considered fit chiefly for the lower classes—"

Tomasz reddened. "Idiots!" he muttered.

"Different worlds, different ways," said Chawker Minor rather hurriedly. "But even then, Grand-Elder, Prime was popular when something was needed that was convenient, inexpensive, and nourishing. And they got their Prime from us. All of them had a fungal strain brought originally from Gammer."

"Which strain?"

"Strain A-5," said Chawker Minor, apologetically. "It's the sturdiest, they said, and the most energy-sparing."

"And the coarsest," said Tomasz, in satisfaction. "And what flavor-additives?"

"Very few," said Chawker Minor. He thought a moment, then said, "There was, on Kapper, a place where they had an additive that was popular with the Kapperpeople and that had—possibilities. Those were not properly developed, however, and when I distributed tastes of what Lady-mine had sent me they were forced to admit that it was to theirs as Gammer is to a space-pebble."

"You had not told me that," said Lady Chawker who, till then, had not ventured to interpose in a conversation that had the Grand-Elder as one of its participants. "The Other-Worlders liked my preparations, did they?"

"I didn't often hand it out," said Chawker Minor. "I was too selfish to do it; but when I did, they liked it a great deal, Lady-mine."

§   §   §

It was several days before the two brothers managed to find a way of being alone together.

Major said, "Weren't you on Kee at all?"

Chawker Minor lowered his voice. "I was. Just a couple of days. It was too expensive to stay long."

"I have no doubt Elder would not have liked even the two days."

"I don't intend telling him. Do you?"

"A witless remark. Tell me about it."

Chawker Minor did, in semi-embarrassed detail, and said, finally, "The point is, Major, it doesn't seem wrong to them. They don't think anything of it. It made me think that perhaps there is no real right and wrong. What you're used to, that's right. What you're not used to, that's wrong."

"Try telling that to Elder."

"What he thinks is right, and what he is used to, are precisely the same. You'll have to admit that."

"What difference does it make what *I* admit? Elder thinks that all rights and wrongs were written down by the makers of Gammer and that it's all in a book of which there is only one copy and we have it, so that all the Other-Worlds are wrong forever. —I'm speaking metaphorically, of course."

"I believe that, too, Major—metaphorically. But it shook me up to see how calmly those Other-World people took it. I could—watch them browse."

A spasm of distaste crossed Major's face. "Animals, you mean?"

"It doesn't look like animals when they browse on it. That's the point."

"You watched them kill, and dissect that—that—"

"No." Hastily. "I just saw it when it was all finished. What they ate looked like some kinds of Prime and it smelled like some kinds of Prime. I imagine it tasted—"

Chawker Major twisted his expression into one of extreme revulsion, and Chawker Minor said, defensively, "But browsing came first, you know. On Earth, I mean. And it could be that when Prime was first developed on Gammer it was designed to imitate the taste of browse-food."

"I prefer not to believe that," said Chawker Major.

"What you prefer doesn't matter."

"Listen," said Chawker Major. "I don't care what

they browse. If they ever got the chance to eat real Prime—not Strain A-5, but the fatted fungus, as the saying goes—and if they had the sophisticated additives and not whatever primitive trash they use, they would eat forever and never dream of browsing. If they could eat what *I* have constructed, and will yet construct—"

Chawker Minor said, wistfully, "are you really going to try for the Award, Major?"

Chawker Major thought for a moment, then said, "I think I will, Minor. I really will. Even if I don't win, I eventually will. This program I've got is different." He grew excited. "It's not like any computer program I've ever seen or heard of; and it works. It's all in the—" But he pulled himself up sharply and said uneasily, "I hope, Minor, you don't mind if I *don't* tell you about it? I haven't told anyone."

Chawker Minor shrugged. "It would be foolish to tell anyone. If you really have a good program, you can make your fortune; you know that. Look at Grand-Elder Tomasz. It must be thirty-five years since he developed Corridor-Song and he still hasn't published his path."

Chawker Major said, "Yes, but there's a pretty good guess as to how he got to it. And it's not really, in my opinion,—" He shook his head doubtfully, in preference to saying anything that might smack of *lèse-majesté*.

Chawker Minor said, "The reason I asked if you were going to try for the Award—"

"Well?"

"Is that I was rather thinking of entering myself."

"You? You're scarcely old enough."

"I'm twenty-two. But would you mind?"

"You don't know enough, Minor. When have you ever handled a computer?"

"What's the difference? A computer isn't the answer."

"No? What is?"

"The taste-buds."

"Hit-and-miss-and-tastebuds-all-the-way. We all know that sound and I will jump through the zero-axis in a bound, too, as the saying goes."

"But I'm serious, Major. A computer is only the starting point, isn't it? It all ends with the tongue no matter where you start."

"And, of course, a Master-Gustator like Minor-lad-here can do it."

Chawker Minor was not too tanned to flush. "Maybe not a Master-Gustator, but a Gustator anyway, and you know it. The point is that being away from home for a year, I've gotten to appreciating good Prime and what might be done with it. I've learned enough—Look, Major, my tongue is all I've got, and I'd like to make back the money that Elder and Lady spent on me. Do you object to my entering? Do you fear the competion?"

Chawker Major stiffened. He was taller and heavier than Chawker Minor and he didn't look friendly. "There is no competition to fear. If you want to enter, do so, Minor-child. But don't come whimpering to me when you're ashamed. And I tell you, Elder won't like your making a no-taste-batch of yourself, as the saying goes."

"Nobody has to win right away. Even if I don't win, I eventually will, as *your* saying goes," and Chawker Minor turned and left. He was feeling a little huffy himself.

§　§　§

Matters trailed off eventually. Everyone seemed to have had enough of the tales of the Other-Worlds. Chawker Minor had described the living animals he had seen for the fiftieth time and denied he had seen any of them killed for the hundredth. He had painted word-pictures of the grain fields and tried to explain what sunshine looked like when it glinted off men and women and buildings and fields, through air that turned a little blue and hazy in the distance. He explained for the two-hundredth time that no, it was not at all like the sunshine effect in the outer viewing-rooms of Gammer (which hardly anyone visited anyway).

And now that it was all over, he rather missed not being stopped in the corridors. He disliked no longer being a celebrity. He felt a little at a loss as he spun the book-film he had grown tired of viewing and tried not to be annoyed with Lady.

He said, "What's the matter, Lady-mine? You haven't smiled all day."

His mother looked up at him, thoughtfully. "It's distressing to see dissension between major and minor."

"Oh, come." Chawker Minor rose irritably and walked over to the air-vent. It was jasmine-day and he loved the odor and, as always, automatically wondered how he could make it better. It was very faint, of course, since everyone knew that strong floral odors blunted the tongue.

"There's nothing wrong, Lady," he said, "with my trying for the Award. It's the free right of every Gammerperson over twenty-one."

"But it isn't in good taste to be competing with your brother."

"Good taste! Why not? I'm competing with everyone. So's he. It's just a detail that we're competing with each other. Why don't you take the attitude that he's competing with me?"

"He's three years older than you, Minor-mine."

"And perhaps he'll win, Lady-mine. He's got the computer. Has Major asked you to get me to drop out?"

"No, he did not. Don't think that of your brother." Lady spoke earnestly, but she avoided his eyes.

Chawker Minor said, "Well, then, he's gone moping after you and you've learned to tell what he wants without his having to say it. And all because I qualified in the opening round and he didn't think I would."

"Anyone can qualify," came Chawker Major's voice

114

from the doorway.

Chawker Minor whirled. "Is that the way it is? Then why does it upset you? And why did a hundred people fail to qualify?"

Chawker Major said, "What some small-taste-nitherlings decide means very little, Minor. Wait till it comes to the board."

"Since you qualified, too, Major, there's no need to tell me how little importance there is to some small-taste-nitherlings—"

"Young-mine," said Lady, rather sharply. "Stop it! Perhaps we can remember that it is very unusual for both Major and Minor of a single unit to qualify."

Neither ventured to break the silence in Lady's presence for a while thereafter—but their scowls remained eloquent.

§ § §

As the days passed, Chawker Minor found himself more and more involved in preparing the ultimate sample of flavored Prime that, his own taste-buds and olfactory area would tell him, were to be nothing like anything that had ever rolled across a Gammer tongue before.

He took it upon himself to visit the Prime vats themselves, where the delectably bland fungi grew out of malodorous wastes and multiplied themselves at extraordinary speed, under carefully idealized conditions, into three dozen basic strains, each in its varieties.

(The Master-Gustator, tasting unflavored Prime itself—the fungal unalterate, as the saying went—could be relied upon to pin its source down to the section and corridor. Grand-Elder Tomasz had more than once stated, publicly, that he could tell the very vat itself and, at times, the portion of the vat, though no one had ever quite put him to the full test.)

Chawker Minor did not pretend to the expertise of Tomasz, but he lipped and tongued and smacked and nipped till he had decided on the exact strain and variety he wanted, the one which would best blend with the ingredients he was mixing in his mind. A good Gustator, said Grand-Elder Tomasz, could combine ingredients mentally and taste the mixture in pure imagination. With Tomasz, it might, for all one knew, be merely a statement, but Chawker Minor took it seriously and was sure he could do it.

He had rented out space in the kitchens (another expense for poor Elder, although Chawker Minor was making do with less than Major had demanded).

Chawker Minor did not repine at having less, for, since he was eschewing computers, he didn't require much. Mincers, mixers, heaters, strainers, and the rest of the cookery tools took up little room. And at least he had an excellent hood for the masking and removal of all odors. (Everyone knew the horror-tales of the Gustators who had been given away by a single sniff of odor and then found that some creative mixture was in the common domain before they could bring it before the board. To steal someone else's product might not be, as Lady would say, in good taste, but it was done and there was no legal recourse.)

The signal-light flashed, in a code sufficiently well-known. It was Elder Chawker. Chawker Minor felt the thrill of guilt he had felt as a child when he had pilfered dabs of Prime reserved for guests.

"One moment, Elder-mine," he sang out, and, in a flurry of activity, set the hood on high, closed the partition, swept his ingredients off the table-top and into the bins, then stepped out and closed the door quickly behind him.

"I'm sorry, Elder-mine," he said, with an attempt at lightness, "but Gustatorship is paramount."

"I understand," said Elder, stiffly, though his nostrils had flared momentarily as though he would have been glad to catch that fugitive whiff, "but you've scarcely been at home lately, scarcely more so than when you were at your space-folly, and I must come here to speak to you."

"No problem, Elder, we'll go to the lounge."

The lounge was not far away and, fortunately, it was empty. Elder's sharp glances this way and that made the emptiness seem fortunate for him and Chawker Minor sighed inaudibly. He would be lectured, he knew.

Elder said, at last, "Minor, you are my son, and I will do my duty toward you. My duty does not consist, however, of more than paying your expenses and seeing to it that you have a fair start in life. There is also the matter of reproval in good time. Who wishes fair Prime must not stint on foul waste, as the saying goes."

Chawker's eyes dropped. He, along with his brother, had been among the thirty who had now qualified for the final Awarding to be held but a week in the future, and, the unofficial rumor had it, Chawker Minor had done so with a somewhat higher score than Chawker Major had.

"Elder," said Chawker Minor, "would you ask me to do less than my best for my brother's sake?"

Elder Chawker's eyes blinked in a moment of puzzlement and Chawker Minor clamped his mouth shut. He had clearly jumped in the wrong direction.

Elder said, "I do not ask you to do less than your best, but rather more than you are doing. Bethink you of the shaming you have inflicted on us in your little onset with Stens Major last week."

Chawker Minor had, for a moment, difficulty remembering what this could apply to. He had done nothing with Stens Major at all—a silly young woman with whom he was perfectly content to confine himself to mere talk, and not very much of that.

"Stens Major? Shaming? How?"

"Do not say you do not remember what you said to her. Stens Major repeated it to her elder and lady, good friends of our family, and it is now common talk in the Section. What possessed you, Minor, to assault the traditions of Gammer?"

"I did not do such a thing. She asked me about my

117

Grand Tour and I told her no more than I have told three hundred others."

"Didn't you tell her that women should be allowed to go on the Grand Tour?"

"Oh."

"Yes. Oh."

"But, Elder, what I said was that if she would take the Grand Tour herself there would be no need to ask questions, and when she pretended to be shocked at such a suggestion, I told her that, in my opinion, the more Gammerpeople saw of the Other-Worlds, the better it would be for all of us. We are too closed a society in my opinion, and Elder, I am not the first to say so."

"Yes, I have heard of radicals who have said so, but not in our Section and certainly not in our family. We have endured longer than the other worlds; we have a stabler and fitter society; we do not have their problems. Is there crime among us? Is there corruption among us?"

"But Elder, it is at the price of immobility and living death. We're all so tied in, so enclosed."

"What can they teach us, these Other-Worlds? Were you not yourself glad to come back to the enclosed and comfortable Sections of Gammer with their corridors lit in the golden light of our own energy?"

"Yes—but, you know, I'm spoiled, too. There are many things on the Other-Worlds that I would have very much liked to have made myself accustomed to."

"And just exactly what, Minor-madman-mine?"

Chawker Minor bit back the words. After a pause, he said, "Why simply make assertions? When I can *prove* that this particular Other-World way or that, is superior to Gammerfashion, I will produce the proof. Till then, what is the use of just talking?"

"You have already been talking idly without end, Minor, and it has done you so little good that we can call what it has done you harm outright. —Minor, if you have any respect left for me after your Grand Tour, which Lady-yours wheedled out of me against

118

my will, Gammer knows, or if you have any regard for the fact that I still deny you nothing that my credit can obtain for you, you will keep your mouth shut, henceforward. Think not that I will halt at sending you away if you shame us. You may then continue on your Grand Tour for as long as the Orbit lasts—and be no son of mine thereafter."

Chawker Minor said in a low voice. "As you say, Elder. From this moment on, unless I have evidence, I will say nothing."

"Since you will never have evidence," said Elder grimly, "I will be satisfied if you keep your word."

§ § §

The annual Finals was the greatest holiday occasion, the greatest social event, the greatest excitement of any sort in the course of the year. Each one of thirty dishes of elegantly-flavored Prime had been prepared. Each one of the thirty judges would taste each dish at intervals long enough to restore the tongue. It would take all day.

In all honesty, Gammerpeople had to admit that the nearly one hundred winners that had taken their prize and acclaim in Gammer history had not all turned out dishes that had entered the Great Menu as classics. Some were forgotten and some were now considered ordinary. On the other hand, at least two of Gammer's all-time favorites, combinations that had been best-sellers in restaurants and homes for two decades, had been also-rans in the years in which they had entered the contest. "Black Velvet," whose odd combination of chocolate-warm and cherry-blossom had made it the standard sweet, did not even make it to the Finals.

Chawker Minor had no doubt of the outcome. He was so confident that he found himself in continual danger of being bored. He kept watching the faces of the individual judges as every once in a while one of them would scoop up a trifle from one of the dishes and place it on his tongue. There was a careful blankness to the expression, a heavy-liddedness to the eye. No true judge could possibly allow a look of surprise or a sigh of satisfaction to escape him—certainly not a quiver of disdain. They merely recorded their ratings on the little computer cards they carried.

Chawker Minor wondered if they could possibly restrain their satisfaction, when they tasted *his*. In the last week, his mixture had grown perfect, had reached a pinnacle of taste-glory that could not be improved on, could *not*—

"Counting your winnings?" said Chawker Major in his ear.

Chawker Minor started, and turned quickly. Chawker Major was dressed entirely in platon and gleamed beautifully.

Chawker Minor said, "Come, Major-mine, I wish you the best. I really do. I want you to place as high as possible."

"Second place if you win, right?"

"Would you refuse second place if I win?"

"You can't win. I've checked somewhat. I know your strain of Prime; I know your ingredients—"

"Have you spent any time on your own work, all this time you've been playing detective?"

"Don't worry about me. It didn't take long to learn that there is no way you can combine your ingredients into anything of value."

"You checked that with the computer, I suppose?"

"I did."

"Then how did I get into the Finals, I wonder? Perhaps you don't know all there is to know about my ingredients. Look, Major, the number of effective combinations of even a few ingredients is astronomical if we consider the various possible proportions and the possible treatments before and after mixing, and the order of mixing and the—"

"I don't need your lecture, Minor."

"Then you know that no computer in existence has been programmed into the complexity of a clever tongue. Listen, you can add some ingredients in

120

amounts so small as to be undetectable even by tongue and yet add a cast of flavor that represents a marked change."

"They teach you that in the Outer-Worlds, youngling?"

"I learned that for myself." And Chawker Minor walked away before he could be goaded into talking too much.

§ § §

There was no question that Grand-Elder Tomasz this year, as in a large number of previous years, held the Judging Committee in the hollow of his tongue, as the saying went.

He looked up and down the long table at which all the judges had now taken their seat in order of preference, with Tomasz himself right in the middle. The computer had been fed; it had produced the result. There was complete silence in the room where the contestants, their friends, and their families sat, waiting for glory and, failing that, for at least the consolation of being able to taste all the contesting samples.

The rest of Gammer, possibly without exceptions, watched by holo-video. There would, after all, be additional batches made up for a week of feasting and the general opinion did not always match that of the judges either, though that did not affect the prize winning.

Tomasz said, "I do not recall an Awarding in which there was so little doubt as to the computer-decision, or such general agreement."

There was a nodding of heads, and smiles and looks of satisfaction.

Chawker Minor thought: They look sincere; not as if they're just going along with the Grand-Elder, so it must be mine.

Tomasz said, "It has been my privilege this year to taste a dish more subtle, more tempting, more ambrosial than anything I have ever, in all my time and experience, tasted. It is the best. I cannot imagine it

being bettered."

He held up the computo-cards, "The win is unanimous and the computer was needed only for the determination of the order of the runners-up. The winner is—" just that pause for effect and then, to the utter surprise of everyone but the winner, "Chawker Minor, for his dish entitled Mountain-Cap. —Young Man."

Chawker Minor advanced for the ribbon, the plaque, the credits, the hand-shakes, the recording, the beaming, and the other contestants received their numbers in the list. Chawker Major was in fifth place.

§ § §

Grand-Elder Tomasz sought out Chawker Minor after a while and tucked the young man's arm into his elbow.

"Well, Chawker Minor, it is a wonderful day for you and for all of us. I did not exaggerate. Your dish

122

was the best I've ever tongued.—And yet you leave me curious and wondering. I identified all the ingredients, but there was no way in which their combinations could produce what was produced. Would you be willing to impart your secret to me? I would not blame you if you refused, but in the case of an accomplishment so towering by one so young, to—"

"I don't mind telling you, Grand-Elder. I intend to tell everybody. I told my Elder that I would say nothing till I had proof. You supplied that proof !"

"What?" said Tomasz, blankly. "What proof ?"

"The idea for the dish occurred to me, actually, on the Other-World Kapper, which is why I called it Mountain-Cap in tribute. I used ordinary ingredients, Grand-Elder, carefully blended, all but one. I suppose you detected the Garden-Tang?"

"Yes, I did, but there was a slight modification there, I think, that I did not follow. How did the Other-World you speak of affect matters?"

"Because it was not Garden-Tang, Grand-Elder, not the chemical. I used a complicated mixture for the Garden-Tang, a mixture of whose nature I cannot be entirely certain."

Tomasz frowned portentiously. "You mean, then, you cannot reproduce this dish?"

"I *can* reproduce it; be certain of that, Grand-Elder. The ingredient to which I refer is garlic."

Tomasz said impatiently, "That is only the vulgar term for Mountain-Tang."

"*Not* Mountain-Tang. That is a known chemical mixture. I am speaking of the bulb of the plant."

Grand-Elder Tomasz's eyes opened wide and so did his mouth.

Chawker Minor continued enthusiastically, "No mixture can duplicate the complexity of a growing product, Grand-Elder, and on Kapper they have grown a particularly delicate variety which they use in their Prime. They use it incorrectly, without any appreciation of its potentiality. I saw at once that a true Gammerperson could do infinitely better, so I brought back with me a number of the bulbs and used them to good advantage. You said it was the best dish of Prime you had ever rolled tongue over and if there is any better evidence than that for the value of opening our society, then—"

But he dwindled to a stop at last, and stared at Tomasz with surprise and alarm. Tomasz was backing away rapidly. He said, in a gargling voice, "A growth—from the dirt—I've eaten—"

The Grand-Elder had often boasted that such was the steadiness of his stomach that he had never vomited, not even in infancy. And certainly no one had ever vomited in the great Hall of Judgment. The Grand-Elder now set a precedent in both respects.

§ § §

Chawker Minor had not recovered. He would never recover. If it were exile that Elder Chawker had pronounced, so be it. He would never return.

Elder had not come to see him off. Neither had Major, of course. It didn't matter. Chawker Minor swore inwardly that he would make out, somehow, without their help, if it meant serving on Kapper as a cook.

Lady *was* there, however, the only one in all the field to see him off; the only one to dare accept the non-person he had become. She shivered and looked mournful and Chawker Minor was filled with the desperate desire to justify himself.

"Lady-mine," he said, in a fury of self-pity, "It's *unfair*! It was the best dish ever made on Gammer. The Grand-Elder said so *himself*. The *best*. If it had grated bulb in it, that didn't mean the dish was bad; it meant the bulb was good. Don't *you* see it? —Look, I must board the ship. Tell me you see it. Don't you understand it means we must become an open society, learn from others as well as teach others, or we'll wither?"

The platform was about to take him up to the ship's entrance. She was watching him sadly, as though she knew she would never see him again.

124

He began the final rise, leaned over the rail. "What did I do *wrong*, Lady-mine?"

And she said in a low, distraught voice, "Can't you see, Minor-mine, that what you did was not in—"

The clang of the ship's-port opening drowned her last two words, and Chawker Minor moved in and put the sight of Gammer behind him forever.

WHEN THERE'S NO MAN AROUND
by Stephen Goldin

*This story's author is 30, has a degree
in astronomy from UCLA, formerly worked
as a physicist for the Navy's space
program, and is now a full-time writer.
His first hardcover SF novel,* Assault
on the Gods, *will be out from Doubleday
soon. Mr. Goldin's hobbies these days
are reading and collecting original-cast
recordings of Broadway musicals. His
wife, Kathleen Sky, who also writes
disapproves of this story; but ...*

"Sandrust!" Lucy Stargos said exasperatedly as she kicked the unfeeling machine for the third time. Neither her ejaculation nor her kick did any good, however. The sand tractor still refused to start.

Outside the insulated tractor dome, the Martian night pressed in with cold fixedness and the stars stared down unabashed, the Martian atmosphere being too thin to work up so much as a legitimate twinkle. Phobos and Deimos were both up, doing their feeble part to illuminate the night Marsscape. And in front of the tractor rose the seven-meter crater wall that the vehicle had stalled on while trying to climb it.

Inside the dome, Lucy paced about as best she could. There wasn't much room for pacing, despite the fact that Martian sand tractors were made to be self-contained units, complete with heating, lighting, and food and water dispensers. They had to be—the Martian climate was quite inhospitable to human endurance. A person with an oxygen mask and an electrically heated suit could survive outside in a Martian night for maybe an hour or more; but the Marsmen had developed a phobia of the 'Outside'. No Marsman would leave a tractor dome except under the direst of emergencies.

Lucy was beginning to consider this a dire emergency. She had a vision of how her father would react. He would tower sixteen feet above her head, perched regally upon his Olympus of parental authority. "Well, young lady, what have you got to say for yourself?" The lightning of divine wrath would flash from his eyes, and small beadlets of thunder would drop from his brow. He would glower a small marsquake at her, and when she didn't say anything he would continue, "I was against letting you have the tractor in the first place. Your mother talked me into it. Personally, I don't think a girl your age should be allowed to go outside the city at night. Especially just to visit that boyfriend of yours. From now on, I smite you with the curse that you're not to go driving unless there's somebody responsible along with you. Understand?" And the specter departed in a flourish of hautboys.

"It's all your fault," Lucy said to the tractor. "What have you got against me, anyhow?"

The tractor merely sat there and politely refused to comment.

"Look, I've got to get back to Syrtis in an hour, or Daddy'll kill me. Come on, now, be a nice tractor and start." She pressed the ignition button again. The motor whirred encouragingly. "Come on, baby," she coaxed it. "Come on." The motor coughed, turned over—and died.

"Darn you!" she screamed at the machine. "Why don't you cooperate?"

The tractor, perhaps unable to think of an excuse, did not answer.

It wouldn't be so bad, Lucy mused, if this had happened on the main road. There was lots of traffic there, and she would easily have been able to find someone to help her. But she had forgotten all about so trivial a thing as time when she was with Jerry, until she'd realized that it was much too late to get home by the time her father had insisted on. "Don't worry," Jerry had said, and the wise patience of the gods had beamed through his Adonis-like face. Then he had presented her with two stone tablets, and inscribed in the living rock were the laws of the Universe. "There is an ancient, secret path that'll get you back in half the time," he went on. "Of course, it's a little bit out of the way...."

A *little bit* out of the way! She had never seen such completely deserted land in all her life. She might as well be at the North Pole for all the help she could expect to get here. Darn Jerry and his silly shortcuts!

Should she try walking? The trouble was, she did not know how far she was from Syrtis. The tractor's odometer read nine hundred and ninety-nine kilometers. It had read nine hundred and ninety-nine kilometers when she'd left Roperston. In fact, for as long as she could remember, it had always read nine hundred and ninety-nine kilometers. The tractor, with characteristic cowardice, was obviously afraid to turn to an even thousand.

She glanced at the outside temperature thermometer. Minus 30° C. No thank you, no walks tonight. She had heard too many stories of people freezing to death trying to walk long distances instead of waiting calmly back at their tractors. That was one reason why the tractor domes were so self-sufficient.

She could see the headlines that would have blazoned forth tomorrow: GIRL FREEZES ATTEMPTING WALK TO SYRTIS.

No, make that **PRETTY GIRL FREEZES ATTEMPTING WALK TO SYRTIS.**

Or better yet,

NOBLE PRETTY GIRL FREEZES ATTEMPTING WALK TO SYRTIS TO SATISFY FATHER'S ARBITRARY DEMAND THAT SHE BE HOME BY MIDNIGHT.

"I guess I'm stuck with you," she informed the tractor. She realized, after she said it, the double meaning of 'stuck', but she was too worried to groan at her own involuntary pun. "Please start this time."

She pressed the ignition button. The motor made a half-hearted attempt, then gave up completely. "You really want Daddy to kill me, don't you. You won't be satisfied until I'm lying there on the living room floor with my skull bashed in and my blood dripping onto the tile in a messy red puddle. But don't forget, that'll make you an accessory to murder. They'll come and take you away to the Home for Wayward Tractors and you'll spend the rest of your days pulling a plow in a cucumber patch."

A thought occurred to her. "I know what. I'll look in the instruction manual, that's what I'll do. That'll fix you." If the tractor was intimidated, however, it hid its fear bravely behind stone silence.

130

She fished the manual out of the map compartment and skimmed to the appropriate passage. " 'If your tractor should by some chance stall,' " she read aloud, " 'it is probably due to a flooding of the gas line. Wait five to ten minutes for the fuel concentration to return to normal, then try the ignition again.' See there, Buster? I've got your number now. Thought you could put one over on ol' Tailspin Lucy Stargos, did you?" she gloated.

To make extra sure, she waited a full fifteen minutes, sucking nervously on a food bar from the dispenser all the while. Finally, when she could take the strain no longer, she pressed the ignition button one more time. There was a discouraging whine, sputter, cough . . . then nothing.

"Darn you!" she shrieked. "I know your type. You just want to lure a pretty, helpless girl out into the middle of nowhere so you can take advantage of her. But I'm not the sort of girl who gives in that easily. You've got a fight on your hands when you mess with me."

She wondered whether she should put her headlights back on and hope that somebody passing nearby would see the glare. But the chances were against anybody passing this deserted spot (darn Jerry!). And anyway, the Martian atmosphere was so thin that it carried glare almost not at all. Even the light from a big city like Syrtis could be lost in the glare of tiny Phobos once you got a hill or two between yourself and the town. In order to see her lights, a person would have to be inside the crater with her, in which case they'd see her anyway. Better not to put a strain on the battery.

"The problem with you," she psychoanalyzed to the tractor, "is that you're ungrateful. I've always taken care of you. Remember when Willie the Creep wanted to race and I told him no, that I had to keep you in good condition? And now, when I need you, this is the thanks I get. Is that fair?"

The tractor looked guilty, but said nothing.

"But my mercy is infinite," she continued with a self-reverent smile. "I'll tell you what I'll do. If you start for me right now, I'll never drive you over twelve kilometers an hour, I'll scrub you down every week, and I'll keep your dome polished like the Universe has never seen. I give you this as my Word, an eternal covenant between us. Is it a deal?" She thumbed the starter.

It was, apparently, not a deal.

Lucy picked up the instruction manual again and turned to the "Repairs" section. " 'Your Carlisle A-7 Sand Tractor will probably not need any repairs for several years, as it is built with the finest . . .' " She skipped down a paragraph. " 'At the first sign of trouble, take the tractor to an authorized repair shop only. *Caution:* any repairs made by a non-authorized shop will invalidate the warranty.' " Since the warranty had lapsed six months ago, this was no great problem. But it was also no great help.

"Well," she said, turning back to the stubborn machine, "do *you* know of any authorized repair shops around here?"

The tractor's silence confessed ignorance.

"Neither do I. So if you don't start this time, Carlisle, I'm going to take you apart myself. Me, old Butterfingers Stargos, who flunked Tinkertoys in kindergarten. So if you want to stay in the condition God intended for you, you'd better work now." The tractor ignored her threat and obstinately refused to start. "So be it," Lucy grunted.

Again owing to the Marsmen's dislike of the Outside, the motor of a Martian sand tractor is made to be accessible from the passenger dome. Removing the plate that covered the engine, Lucy sat down and stared at her foe face-to-face for the first time. The sight of the wires and filters, carburetor and camshaft, sparkplugs and battery was dismaying, but she resolved not to show her doubts. "I'll give you one last chance to reason this thing out," she said. "Don't you want to get back safe and sound into your nice warm garage, instead of sitting out here at thirty below? I promise that, first thing tomorrow, I'll have you looked at by the best mechanic on Mars. It'll set me back three months' allowance, but I'll do it 'cause I'm basically a nice guy. How about it?"

The haughty motor did not deign to reply.

"Okay, Carlisle, I've gone easy on you so far because I wanted to save us both a lot of trouble. But I can see now that I've been wasting my time—all you understand is sheer brute force. You were built by human beings, right?"

The machine was noncommittal.

"Okay, what one human being can build, another can fix. I am going to vivisect you, my dear Carlisle, until I find out what's wrong. What do you say to that?"

The shocked motor was speechless.

And still Lucy hesitated. She had not the faintest idea of how to take an engine apart, let alone put it together again. But the motor stared back at her defiantly, and she knew that she couldn't let herself be bluffed down.

There was one wire toward the back that looked as though it might have come loose. She reached in to tighten it—

ZZZSST.

She pulled her hand back sharply and bumped her elbow on a seat. "Damn!" she screamed, then looked around involuntarily to make sure that no one had heard her unladylike expletive.

"So that's how you're going to play it!" she shrieked at the machine, which seemed to be smirking. "All right, from now on it's no more Miss Nice Guy. If you want war, that's what you'll get. Starraker Stargos rides again!"

She tore into the hapless motor with a vengeance. Wires, sparkplugs, battery caps, filter covers, and anything else that was the slightest bit loose yielded before her furious assault. Within minutes, she was surrounded by her captured booty, and she smiled triumphantly at the once-proud engine, now denuded and humble. "That'll teach you," she declared with finality.

Her moment of glory was short-lived, however, as she came to the realization that she was no better off than she'd been before. Worse, in fact, since she wasn't at all sure how to put things back together again. She glowered at the motor and said through gritted teeth, "You tricked me!"

She stole a glance at the clock on the dashboard. Eleven-thirty. Only half an hour now separated her from the Moment of Paternal Doom. And here she sat in a useless sand tractor in the middle of a cold Martian night, probably millions of kilometers from anywhere, with no possible chance of rescue.

"Doomed," she intoned, with all the melodramatics of her junior-grade drama class at her disposal. "Doomed to die alone and unloved in an alien desert. Sent here to perish by my witless lover, spurned by my arrogant father, failed even by my faithful Carlisle A-7 Sand Tractor. In a little while it shall all be over. Thirst will dry my mouth and crack my lips. Hunger will shrivel my stomach. I will lie here, parched and famished, until all life escapes me. And the flesh will rot on my bones, and the air in this dome will be filled with the malodorous stench of decomposing carrion. And when my body is finally discovered, a century from now, they will know who I am by my tarnished and faded ID bracelet. They will wail and bemoan my fate, that I died so young without tasting the succulent fruits of life, and they'll sing songs of mourning and compose ballads of sadness for this pathetic creature who dies here today." With remarkable control of her tear ducts, she let fall a single saline drop from her right eye.

Then, in this hour of her greatest trial, she remembered what her mother had told her many years ago when the toaster blew up. "Life is not easy for a woman, Lucy. There are always men, poor darlings, to be looked after, or they're sure to be in some kind of trouble. But even worse is that insidious creation of man—Machine. There is the real enemy, don't ever forget it. The war between Machine and Woman-kind is ages old, and will end only with the exter-mination of one or the other of the species. But in this struggle, we have one Weapon that has never failed us." And she had proceeded to demonstrate by fixing the toaster unassisted in a matter of minutes.

Lucy sighed. The time had indeed come for the Ul-timate Weapon. Reaching up into her hair, she pulled out a bobby pin. . . .

Ten minutes later, the job was done. Lucy Stargos replaced the engine cover and faced the dashboard. Sweat was gathering on her palms, and she wiped them nervously on her blouse. The moment of truth had arrived. Long-dead generations of women peered over her shoulder hopefully as she gently caressed the ignition button like a reluctant lover. Until at last she could stand the suspense no longer and pushed it eagerly.

The tractor, defeated at last, hummed to life. Lucy squealed with pure joy at the thought that, once again, Woman had triumphed over Machine. Those long-dead watchers sighed with relief and returned to their other pursuits.

"Onward, Carlisle," Lucy said, cracking an imagi-nary whip. "Onward and upward." As the tractor surged ahead, Lucy looked at the dashboard clock. Fifteen minutes to go. If she drove at top speed, she might not be too late. With any luck . . .

She topped the rim of the crater and saw the lights of Syrtis glaring mockingly at her barely a thousand meters away.

Lucy Stargos's next reaction was far from ladylike.

IN DARKNESS WAITING
by Stephen Leigh

Although the author of "In Darkness Waiting" has a degree in art education, he works full time as a musician, with occasional windfalls from writing and artwork. Mr. Leigh, now 25, has been writing with intent to sell for about three years, and is now beginning to see regular publication. He's currently working (slowly, he says) on a novel. He and his wife live near Cincinnati.

Pause. And shiveringly inhale. Grudging air for complaining lungs.

The quarry was just ahead. The two assassins increased their pace. Night-quiet, the Hoorka advanced, like shadows unseen in overlying murk and as deadly as the wind-spiders of the western tundra.

It was twenty minutes till dawn.

They were running now, the Hoorka.

They halted in the comforting darkness cast by a high porch. Somewhere ahead, their victim was enmeshed in the thick metal pilings that held the houses above the early rains and the cold floods that inevitably followed. These were the tenements, the most temporary section of a city that had not been meant by its creators to last more than fifty years and was now in its second century. Wooden beams lent support to the time- and rust-weakened pillars of metal. Decay, an odor formed of river mud and rust, filled their quickly flaring nostrils.

Aldhelm, the taller of the Hoorka, could see the man now. The victim was breathing heavily, his right arm extended above his head as he leaned against the understructure of a house. His head was bowed, his knees slightly bent. The muck caked his shoes—he'd been easy to follow.

The ooze glistened coldly with slats of blue-white light. The seams of the flooring overhead grinned with age. Aldhelm could hear the indistinct rise and fall of murmured conversation above him, punctuate unevenly by his breathing and his companion's. The voices discussed the abundance of sandmites as the two Hoorka moved below them.

The mud that had so clearly marked their man's flight also saved him. Even the assassins of Hoorka, adept at silentstalk, were not immune to mud. The river filth sucked greedily at the soles of their feet, relinquishing them with a liquid protest. Their intended victim's head snapped up; they were still thirty meters from him, under the next dwelling. He ducked instinctively, and the Khaelian-made dagger only creased him, drawing a burning line from shoulder to mid-back before burying its ultra-hard point twenty millimeters into the metal pillar behind him. Even as he looked, it began to wriggle and loosen, the electronic devices in it seeking to return to the homing pulse from the Hoorka. He floundered to his feet and ran, weaving from pillar to pillar.

(And Aldhelm cursed under his breath, reproaching the Goddess of Chaos for tipping the scales of chance, praying that she would hold back the sun; for dawn, by the Hoorka code, would give the man life.)

They knew the man would be praying for light, for the imminent sunrise, as that was his sign that the Hoorka's contract had run its twelve hour length and—unmoved, uncaring—they would permit him to live. Already the morning sky was luminous with promise. The Hoorka moved quickly.

Aldhelm loosed another dagger. It clattered from a pillar and, twirling, struck the man handle foremost. Silver glimmered as the weapon turned and arced back to the Hoorka.

Pursued and pursuers ran, ignoring the banded pain that constricted their chests and stabbed in their lungs. Another knife was released; it clanged against a pillar at the man's right. He feinted left and dove to his right as a Hoorka blade fountained mud at his feet. He slipped, coating himself with umber goo, and regained his footing. The stench of decaying vegetation made him gag, and he slipped again, retching and struggling. Mud blinded him. He scrabbled frantically at this face.

The Hoorka stood over him now. He lay there, and they watched him flailing in panic, knowing he could feel the pressure of their gaze, knowing he was waiting for the cold blade piercing his body, thrusting deep into his entrails.

Dawn had come, pallid light on a mist-filled morning.

They helped him to his feet, grunting with his limp weight.

"Come on, dammit. You can stand." Aldhelm's voice was neither ice nor fire, not devoid of emotion, but rather so full of it that the individual emotions were indistinguishable.

They watched composure slowly return to the man before them. He wiped vainly at his clothing.

Aldhelm spoke again. "Our admiration, Gunnar. Your life is your own again." His voice, without inflection, spoke the ritual completing the ceremony. "You may go with the light."

For a moment his eyes glinted in the dawnlight, then the Hoorka-assassins turned and were gone, slipping into the near-gloom of Undercity.

The man, Gunnar, stood: dripping, gasping, and covered with filth, confused and thankful, both. He walked slowly away.

§ § §

The Hoorka-thane was possessed by the closest approximation of rage any had ever seen in him.

"Gunnar simply escaped, you say. Unarmed. You let him live until dawn. Two Hoorka let simple prey escape them." His voice was laced with mock surprise that raked the two men standing before him. "Do you both need training in the rudiments? I won't stand for it, not now; I won't have us destroyed by incompetence. You, Aldhelm,"—the Thane turned and glared—"you're the best knife man on the Hoorka Council. How could you let this happen?"

The two looked silently at the Thane. His last

140

words came redundantly back to them, an echo from the far walls of the cavern in which they stood. Lamps glistened from water-filmed rocks and ruddied their complexions, making deep hollows of their eyes. Underasgard. Hoorka-refuge. The caverns.

A vibroblade gleamed sharply in the Thane's hand. He advanced on the two, point foremost. They didn't move.

"Do the two of you realize what you've done? When I began here, we were considered outlaws, no better than petty thugs. I spent years setting this up, gaining us grudging respect, making this an organization protected by the Assembly and tolerated by the Alliance. Idiots!"

The vibro swept before their eyes. The following wind cut them coldly.

"The Li-Gallant Vingi himself signed that contract. Gunnar's death would have left the opposition party in shambles—and Vingi would have had control of the Assembly. Fools!" The Thane gesticulated violently, and the vibro tip gashed Aldhelm's cheek. Blood ran freely, but there was no grimace, no sign of pain. The Thane cursed himself inwardly: he shouldn't have drawn blood then, let himself get so angry with Aldhelm. Are you getting so old, so stupid?, he asked himself. None of this showed in his face.

"You're both out of rotation until further notice. You'll do apprentice work if that's all you're capable of. Aldhelm, I have a contract. You'll take my partner's place. I want to see you work.

"An elementary lesson, children. We're but one step removed from outlaws. No world of the Alliance accepts us, and only this one backwater world allows us to work. We're free despite the fact we've no loyalty to those in power—because the World Assembly and the Alliance know we follow the code. *My* code. We have scruples: we can be trusted to side with no man and no cause. We're society's carnivores, feeding on death without caring what beast provides the

141

meal. Do you see what the Li-Gallant must be thinking? That we let Gunnar escape because we've allied ourselves with him. That's what he thinks. We've lost our faith. Bunglers!"

The Thane shoved the vibro into its scabbard. The leather, blackened with age, showed much use. "Wipe your face, Aldhelm. I should have you both cast out for last night. It's good we're friends and that I have much respect for your earlier work, Aldhelm. It appeases my anger somewhat." His voice might have softened: his dark eyes hadn't. Aldhelm daubed at the blood with the sleeve of his nightcloak. The Thane breathed noisily, immersed in hidden guilt, while the dank caverns amplified the sound. He stroked his beard as the lamps coaxed red highlights from his graying hair. "Extra knife work for the two of you. At least you followed the dawn code. The Alliance might have been watching. I'll try to redeem us, if I can. Go."

They turned. As Aldhelm reached the door, the Thane called to him, prodded by his conscience. Aldhelm turned and looked back, his eyes cold.

"I didn't mean to cut you. I was angry."

Aldhelm shrugged. "I understand." He went through the door that separated this cavern from the others, shut it, and was gone. The memory of Aldhelm's frigid eyes remained with the Thane for a long time.

§ § §

"He did what?"

The Hoorka-thane's face didn't flinch from the shouted query. He didn't move from his seated position, nor did his eyes widen. When he spoke in answer, it was with distilled calm. "He survived. Gunnar lived until dawn. I can't put it more simply for you, Li-Gallant."

Vingi backed away from the assassin. His face screamed anger, but his body sought the comforting bulwark of his desk, putting it between the Hoorka and himself. The lassitude the Hoorka affected in

142

creased Vingi's nervousness.

"You followed my orders?"

"We followed our code. You've read the contract. The victim must have his chance. We're not murderers, you remember. We tilt the scales of death and life, but we aren't gods, nor do we attempt to be."

Vingi expelled irritated breath. Damn them for their ethics, he thought. "What weapons did you use?"

"Daggers from Khaelia. The Alliance brought them to us in payment for a contract a few months ago. Very effective."

"Really?" Vingi waited for a reaction to his sarcasm, and received none. "Why didn't you use firearms?"

"Li-Gallant, Gunnar had no bodyshield. The odds would have been too great. Again, we don't control anyone's life or death. If a person dies by the hand of Hoorka, then he wasn't meant for survival. If he escapes, that indicates he was meant to live. The weak fall; the strong—perhaps—live. If that's cruel, it's no crueler than Fate herself." The Thane's eyes glittered, daring objection. His hands stayed unmoving, folded on the grey-black cloth of his lap.

"I should have sent my own men." Vingi's right hand made a bejeweled fist that hovered indecisively over the marbled desktop. The fist was a weapon of impotence, showing too much disuse to be a symbol of anything but wealth. The Thane's lips curled in a vestige of a smile that flickered for an instant and was gone.

"You sent your own men twice, Li-Gallant. They failed. We check our clients thoroughly."

Vingi grimaced. The raised fist struck the desk with soft anger. "Almost."

"They killed Gunnar's mistress, I believe." The Hoorka's voice seemed devoid of any emotion, but behind the words was contempt.

"That was unfortunate, but unavoidable." Vingi shrugged. The cloth of his robe glistened with interwoven metallic strands.

The Hoorka-thane allowed himself another brief second of amusement. That fabric would turn back the sting of most weapons, and he was certain that when he'd arrived he'd been surreptitiously searched. Beamed and probed. He also knew that if he intended to kill the obese man before him, he wouldn't need any weapons but his own hands. The Li-Gallant distrusted him, even knowing that the Hoorka never killed unless contracted, and never without warning. A bad omen.

"You have our payment, I suppose?"

Vingi's face was a rictus, a snarl. "You demand a high price for small results."

"You know our code." There was no apology in the Thane's voice. Yet he knew this was a dangerous moment, that what he did here might affect Hoorka greatly; and for a moment he was uncertain.

"I've registered a complaint with the Assembly." There was a triumphant sneer on Vingi's face, a vestige of bravado. "You're to come before them tomorrow to answer questions. The Alliance Regent will be there also."

"You accuse us . . . ?"

"You must admit it seems suspicious."

"It would not be wise nor prudent to neglect our payment, Li-Gallant." The Thane stood abruptly, and Vingi started, his eyes wide. Had he made the right move; had he gauged Vingi correctly? If not—he thrust the apprehension from him.

"Are you threatening me?"

The Thane said nothing. In the silence, a muffled voice could be heard in Vingi's outer office, a high clear laugh.

The Li-Gallant slid a pastel cheque across his desk. The Hoorka-thane leaned forward to take it.

"Our thanks, Li-Gallant. Tomorrow, then."

§ § §

The Hoorka-thane walked easily through the streets: easily because the throng parted before him with an apprehensive glance at the grey and black nightcloak of the Assassins' Guild. Grey and black: no colors, no loyalty except to Hoorka-kin. The aura of the Deathgods hung about him, subtle and menacing. They were used to hardship and death, the people of this ghetto world; but the Hoorka were hardened and deadly beyond the norm. Better he be avoided.

The cheque from the Li-Gallant gave the Thane scant pleasure. He had expected avoidance of payment, some hedging at least. But Vingi had been truly angry and would exorcise that anger. How? The question nagged at him.

The populace bustled about him. Someone brushed his side then stammered a quick, frightened apology and hastened away. The Thane noted a few flashily clothed Alliance people from the Port upriver, but even they, the aristocracy protected by the offworld power of the Alliance, gave him wide berth. The Thane walked slowly, thinking—

—the Li-Gallant wants Gunnar dead, and he wants to know whether the Hoorka have sided against him. How will he go about determining that?

—what's wrong? Once I would have reveled in a confrontation like this. Now I'm simply tired and unsure. The old thought: is it time to step aside? Should Aldhelm or Mondom or someone else be Thane?

—it's a good day. The sunstar shines. But my frown puzzles these people. Do they think I contemplate my next contract?

—must rest before tonight's undertaking. Perhaps Shelia—

He touched the pouch in which the cheque rode and smiled, forcibly evicting his pessimism. Passersby shook their heads at the evil omen.

The Hoorka smile only at death.

§ § §

It was another petty vengeance. An influential businessman from an outlying district wanted to dispose of his wife's lover. The Hoorka price was normally too high for such domestic vendettas, but the husband was rich and willing to spend. The Hoorka had offered the usual option, but the rival couldn't match the fee and thus void the contract. Five hours before sunset, he was given the traditional warning and a watch was set.

All this unfolded while the Thane and Aldhelm slept in Underasgard. For such routine, the apprentices were used.

An hour before sundown, word came to Underasgard that the victim had purchased a handgun from a weapon store. Bodyshields were set out and the two Hoorka awakened. Final reports came as they were preparing to leave the caverns. The victim had paid a last visit to the contractor's wife. The victim had headed south from his city. The victim had turned west and fled toward the Twisted Hills. Rope and heavy footgear were added to the assassins' equipment.

The Thane didn't speak until they were alone and the Hills lay before them, silvered in the light of the double moons. The night bore the chill of approaching winter, and both he and Aldhelm kept their nightcloaks gathered tightly about them. A few nightstalkers mewled and shrieked their hunting cries, but otherwise the landscape was lifeless.

"What did our last report say, Aldhelm?" The Thane scanned the barren slopes, seeing nothing but the scraggling, half-dead desert brush. The night was arid, and his throat was parched, as if the air itself leached him of moisture. He tried vainly to work up enough saliva to spit.

Aldhelm squinted into darkness. "The apprentices swear the victim's hidden himself in the foothills just south of here." He swung his hand in that direction, the nightcloak rustling. To the Thane, he was a deeper darkness against the night sky, his flesh dark and his mouth concealed in the folds of the cloak. Only his eyes and the crusted wound on his upper cheek were clearly visible.

"What's your suggestion."

"Go around him. If he expects us from the direction of the town, fine. Come the opposite way."

"Good." Even as he said it, the Thane knew it was wrong. It was patronizing, belittling.

"I'm not an apprentice or a journeyman, Thane. I haven't your age, but I have been Hoorka for some time, if you recall?" His voice was haughty and irritated and the words cut the Thane. Aldhelm was staring into the shadowed valleys of the Hills. "Let's go, Thane."

"Not till we settle this. Speak your mind."

Aldhelm looked at the Thane with eyes that glinted from the darkness of his face.

"Why'd you pull me out of rotation? Wasn't it enough that I failed in the Gunnar contract? Do you have to humiliate me by treating me like a rank newcomer?" He uttered a short and bitter expletive.

The Thane met his gaze and held it. Neither flinched.

"What did you expect? I had to emphasize to all Hoorka the delicacy of our position. The word, that I found it necessary to discipline *you*, the best Hoorka I have, man or woman, will spread. It's the most convincing evidence that we do not conspire with Gunnar." So simplistic, he thought. The words don't even convince me. What can they do for Aldhelm?

Aldhelm spread his arms wide. "So I'm reduced to being an example in your textbook." His voice quivered with menace, and for the first time the Thane was aware of the other's sheer bulk, of his physical condition. In his younger days, he could have taken Aldhelm, he knew, but now... He was no longer sure.

Aldhelm swept his hands through the cold air in disgust, breaking the locked gaze; he turned to stare moodily at the surrounding hills.

There was no sympathy in the Thane's voice when he spoke. His voice was iron, tempered and made steel. It echoed faintly from the hills.

"I've thought of you as my successor, and I've called you a friend. You've become the best of Hoorka, better than I could ever have been. But—" The Thane placed a hand on Aldhelm's shoulder and forced Aldhelm to look at him. "I'd throw you to Vingi's men tied hand and foot if it would save Hoorka. My life is Hoorka. So is yours. I won't have that destroyed, no matter what the sacrifice. Do you understand?"

Aldhelm brushed the Thane's hand from his shoulder. "Perhaps better than you think." He turned and began moving into the hills, the sparse night dew from the brush beading on his nightcloak. He pivoted to face the Thane again. "I understand your reasoning and your motives. As to your claim of friendship, I don't believe you capable of it." He walked away. "I don't like it," he said to the shadowed emptiness ahead.

§ § §

Fulfillment of the contract was routine and simple. They found their prey seated behind a sheltering rock and looking toward the glow on the horizon that bespoke the presence of the city. His head swept the plain in search of movement without noticing the two Hoorka looking down from the heights behind him. The barrel of his weapon glistened in the twin moons' light. He coughed once, and the sound echoed around him.

Aldhelm kicked a pebble downslope, deliberately, and as the man turned, threw a dagger. It sped true. The man crumpled without a cry, the gun still in his hands. Simply, quickly, it was over. The assassins moved toward the body.

"Good work, Aldhelm." The other disdained to reply. "Turn him over. I want to look at him."

"Doesn't your fourth code line say that the Hoorka must show no concern for the victim, must consider him dead once the warning is given, so we can feel no pity?"

"A minor quirk of mine, Aldhelm. I like to see

their faces." The Thane was irritated and let it show.

Aldhelm turned the body with his foot. Moonlight washed the contorted features of the victim's face and outlined the edges of the death-rictus. A thickened rivulet of blood trickled from the corner of his mouth and across his cheek. The hands clasped the useless weapon. It was a common face, a crowd-face.

"Fine. Let's finish this."

They wrapped the body in an extra nightcloak and began the long trek to the contractor's housing, the body a limp weight between them.

It was still early night when they entered the town. The bars were full, the shops open, holos flaring in visual cacophony. The streets were busy, but all moved aside for the impassive Hoorka and their burden. The assassins walked slowly without speaking, their eyes focused on the walkway ahead, and the populace moved to escape their notice. A crowd gathered quickly behind them and when they finally deposited their victim on the contractor's porch, they had attracted a sizable portion of the nightdwellers. These parted silently as the assassins turned to go, then closed in again, clamoring excitedly around the corpse. The Hoorka left, as calmly and unemotionally as they'd come.

(For is it not the sixth code-line that states that both the signing and fulfillment of a contract must be public knowledge, that the Hoorka will make known both the slain and the slayer? For the Hoorka are but tools in the hands of another, and the contractor may himself become the hunted. Revenge is a powerful emotion.)

Back in Underasgard, they slept; the Thane, fitfully. The spectre of the morrow tortured him with an old, old face, channeled and furrowed, dancing a macabre arabesque, wearing the swollen and malevolent visage of Vingi.

§ § §

The Assembly met in a large hall on Port property. Legally, it was Alliance territory and emphasized the

149

control the Alliance wielded over the colony. The room itself was opulent; in another age, it might have been called decadent. It was resplendent with gilt and lavishly furnished: scarlet hangings on the wall, a mosaic of tiles on the floor. It was also well guarded. The Alliance saw to it that none spoiled the effect of rowdiness. Reverence was carefully maintained. The lack of it meant ejection. The hall was deliberately designed to dominate the people it held, and it did so with massive nonfunctional beams glittering with inlay, a distant ceiling that seemed unreachable. Artificial lighting was used only on the dais where the colonial Assembly sat, generally looking cowed and uncomfortable. The remainder of the hall was marbled with alternating swathes of sunlight from the rectangular slashes of windows and mild shadow.

The Thane was met at the Port entrance by an armed escort, and together they walked into the Hall. Even before they entered the main room, the Thane knew it would be filled to capacity. The insect hum of many voices filled the corridor, and an overflow of people was gathered about the huge doors that swung into the Assembly hall. All meetings of the Assembly were open to the public as a matter of course—the Alliance placed that stipulation on use of its facilities by the local government—but like most political functions, they were rarely well attended. Evidently news that the Hoorka were to be examined had spread and had drawn the curious, the morbid, and those who hated Hoorka. The Thane adjusted his cloak about him, readying himself for the assault of stares, but the guard's hand touched him lightly on an elbow, guiding him away from the hall and down a deserted corridor. The sound of voices faded slowly away. They stopped outside an unmarked door, and the escort opened it, motioning the Thane to enter. His muscles tense despite himself, he did.

There were three people within, gathered about a table in the otherwise empty room: Li-Gallant Vingi,

150

the Alliance Regent, and another man that the Thane recognized as a member of Gunnar's political party. The Thane nodded to the Regent. He failed to recognize her—they were replaced so often—and he hoped she knew of the contract the Hoorka had completed for the Alliance, the contract that had netted them the Khaelian daggers. Eventually, he thought, the Hoorka will go offworld, and we'll need Alliance support; much is at stake today.

The Thane seated himself, ignoring the presence of Vingi and of Gunnar's Assemblyman, directing all his attention to the Regent. She appeared impatient. Her lips were taut and drawn, her posture was rigid. She looked as if she might rise and stalk off at any moment. The Thane briefly wondered if there was any way he could use that to his advantage, but cast the thought aside, not willing to trust his instincts, knowing that the Alliance people were skilled in psychological deception. He felt anger at the thought—the Hoorka were not used to being manipulated.

The Thane examined his calloused hands.

Vingi spoke. "The Regent has asked that this be a private meeting rather than a full Assembly meeting, a request that I bowed to, considering that this is not an official trial, nor do I register a formal complaint at this time. Thane, I'm sure you recognize Assemblyman Potok. The Regent wished the opposition party to be represented. And this is m'Dame d'Embry, the Alliance Regent. She—"

"Hold, Li-Gallant." The Regent spoke suddenly and coldly, her eyes boring into Vingi's. The pupils were grey, the Thane noticed, as frigid as the void. For the first time, he allowed himself to relax, if slightly. If the Regent wasn't actively on his side, neither was she on Vingi's. "Everyone here is aware of the situation. I'm interested only in the Assassins' Guild's credibility, and my ship lifts in an hour. Waste no more of my time." Cold, always cold. Does it come from erecting an Alliance from the scattered ashes of a dead empire?, the Thane wondered. They were all like that, these men and women of the Alliance Diplomatic Resources Team.

The Li-Gallant accepted the rebuff with a curt nod. He again cleared his throat. "To the point then. Isn't it true, Thane, that Gunnar escaped from two Hoorka while totally unarmed? Unarmed, mind you—No don't interrupt." The Thane hadn't moved or spoken. "Now, doesn't that seem at least odd and certainly suspicious?"

The Thane glanced at the Regent.

She shrugged and rested her chin on her cupped hand.

The Thane leaned back in his chair. "It's true that Gunnar escaped, as you say. That's hardly in dispute. But you forget, Li-Gallant, that it's part of the Hoorka code that the victim retains the possibility of escape. We contract only to attempt an assassination, and our efforts cease with the light. Gunnar was intelligent and agile enough to elude my people. It was *not* conspiracy. Anyone can escape the Hoorka, if he is fit to survive."

"I paid, Hoorka. I paid for that man's death," Vingi insisted.

The Thane glanced at Potok, who was watching intently. "Death is not for any man to buy." He steepled his hands.

Unconcerned, always unconcerned.

"You're dangerous if you've allied yourself with Gunnar," said Vingi. "I make no pretext of enjoying the presence of members of his party on the Assembly"—this with a glare at Potok that the other returned— "as it only impedes this world's progress, but an alliance of Hoorka with Gunnar would betoken open rebellion. I would have no choice."

Unexpectedly, the Regent broke in, her voice low and steady. "Li-Gallant, you should realize that the Alliance will work with anyone in power here. It makes no difference from our standpoint whether you or Gunnar rules here. We're concerned only with aspects of your world that touch upon others in the Alliance, and what is important here is the ramifications of the Hoorka's having placed themselves in a position of support.

"Your men filled a contract for the Port authorities, if I recall correctly." Her head slowly came around until it faced the Thane. He realized belatedly that the last statement had been addressed to him.

"We were paid in weaponry to attempt to remove a saboteur. It was successful. I remember."

The Terran altered her position in her chair slightly, a quick and sure movement. It was incongruous, compared to her slow speech and deliberate gestures. He wondered how else he'd underestimated her complexities.

"We've considered allowing the Hoorka to accept offworld contracts, but this matter needs to be settled. There are worlds where it's possible your modified savagery could be accepted, and perhaps useful. There are questions also. Can the Hoorka maintain cohesiveness on a larger scale? Perhaps you'll have to limit contracts, and in that case, what determines acceptance or nonacceptance? The whole question of integrity would have larger scope. Can the Hoorka maintain the paramilitary regimentation that seems to be the only thing between them and chaos? Those are things to be answered when you are transplanted offworld, if that happens, and obviously it is something that cannot be rushed. But let's first settle this small quarrel. If the Hoorka cannot function on one small world, then certainly they cannot on several." There was haughtiness in that voice, the ingrained superiority of civilization to the rural, the backward.

"Our kind is not unknown historically, even on the Homeworld. Recall the Thuggee, practiced in ancient India."

"I don't know it. It's of little importance, anyway. Your particular commodity's useless if it becomes linked to any cause."

"If I may be allowed a comment," interjected Potok. He had, till that time, been watching the argument, slumped deep into the yielding caress of the chair. He spoke from the same position. "I'm perhaps closer to the problem than even Vingi. It was, after all, my leader who was the target."

"Nothing can be proved," said the Thane. "I say Gunnar simply escaped us, as some will, and Vingi claims he was set free. We can argue the point all day, if we care to."

Potok slid even deeper into the recesses of the chair. His voice came from somewhere in his upper body. He seemed totally relaxed, and because of that, certain of himself. "My own contribution to this meeting is to state that the Hoorka have not allied themselves with us. I've no love for them—Gunnar was almost killed—but they are fair. I'll grant them that. If I were less scrupulous myself, I might be tempted to say that they had allied themselves, simply because that would destroy them and erase any future threat to my organization from them. My words should have some weight, m'Dame and Li-Gallant."

There were innuendos, shadows of meanings coloring the words. The Thane felt helpless. Does he say that, hoping that he won't be believed, since it is the obvious thing for him to say if we had made a pact with them? Does he say it hoping that we will feel indebted and perhaps be swayed at some future time? Is it simply that he wishes to contradict Vingi, to hinder the Li-Gallant? He shook his head slightly, wondering where the confidence he'd once had during crises had gone.

"It seems an odd time for you to fail a contract, Thane, considering its importance," said Vingi.

You're right. The thought roared in the Thane's head. You're right. Perhaps there should have been no escape, even if it meant violation of the Dawn code. But what use then are ethics? "I would consider that an argument in our favor. Even realizing the consequences, we followed our code."

"Li-Gallant," the Regent said, turning to Vingi, "you mentioned to me earlier that you had a plan to shed further light on the issue."

"I do, m'Dame."

"Good. Then I'll waste no more time here with semantic games." The Regent rose. The Thane remained seated while Vingi and Potok stood. "Since you've managed to fritter away my morning inconclusively, Li-Gallant, I hope your plan bears ripened fruit. I shall be interested in the results." She stared at the Thane for a long moment. "If the Hoorka cannot be interdicted, perhaps you and I shall talk further."

M'Dame d'Embry, in a rustling of glowcloth, left the room.

§ § §

"We have very little choice."

It was the eternal night of Underasgard. Glowtorches guttered fitfully in wall holders. The Thane, Aldhelm, and a few other Hoorka sat around a rough wooden table. Mugs filled with mead sat like islands in shimmering puddles and a pitcher dripped golden liquid within easy reach.

"We can guess Vingi's plan." Aldhelm sipped from his mug slowly. The slash on his cheek was ruddy in torchlight. "I suspect he'll give us a second chance at Gunnar. If so, we can't fail."

"Even if it means abandoning the code?" The speaker, a lithe young woman further down the table, was Mondom. She was generally placed third in the Hoorka hierarchy.

Aldhelm slapped his mug back on the table. Liquid sloshed over the edge of the glass and pooled on the wood. "Yes, in a word."

"No." The Thane was emphatic. "If we violate the code, we've lost our integrity just as Vingi claims. Everything we've set up would be a sham, and . . ."

Aldhelm broke in, slashing his arm through the air. "It becomes a matter of survival. We stand by the code, but if it threatens to force us to fail again, we've got to be prepared to break it. Do you see, Thane? We break the code and live with our guilt, or we die."

"I see your reasoning, but I can't agree. The code is my creation but not even I am free to break it. It's the lifeblood of Hoorka, and we can't taint it. Sometimes the creation must transcend even the creator."

Again Aldhelm's arm slashed. What had started as a meeting was becoming an argument, and the other Hoorka watched in silence, waiting. "I agree. The creation becomes more important, and to insure its safety, we have to do something, even to ignoring the advice of the creator. If Vingi feels he has proof to link us with Gunnar, he'll not only have the Assembly outlaw Hoorka, but he'll have every assassin hunted down and executed for conspiracy, and the Alliance Regent won't stop him. She won't interfere with local politics unless she stands to gain something by it. She's playing a game of patience, waiting to see if we're what we claim to be."

"And you want us to deny what we live by."

"Death will come if we don't. Look at the facts, man!" Aldhelm slammed his fist on the table and shot to his feet. He stalked across the small room, turning at the door. His voice was low and tense with emotion. "Whatever Li-Gallant's contract is, we fulfill it. That's my advice, and others here agree with me, I know." His index finger raked the air, pointing at each of them. "Otherwise Hoorka die and become scum."

§ § §

Sleep never really came that night to the Thane. He hovered in the twilight between sleep and waking, drifting back and forth on some tidal flow he couldn't control. His thoughts were chaotic, formless, as impossible to hold onto as the chimera of sleep. He lay there, his eyes closed to the grey roof of Underasgard, thinking.

He saw the knife arcing toward Aldhelm's face in

aching slowness, haloed with silver reflections, and though he tried, he couldn't hold it back or turn it aside. It cut the flesh, leaving a gash that grinned white and bloodless for a moment before scarlet welled up and flowed. He could only mutter over and over that he was sorry.

He was sorry that he was so unsure. The rest of the meeting had gone badly. Only Mondom had seemed sure of herself, and she defended the code. The others . . . they didn't know. Could it be that it was necessary to sacrifice principles, that survival depended upon knowing when to cast aside the rules?

No one could tell him where he should go. He was young again, just dismissed from the task force that had joined in the rebellion that followed the suicide-death of the dictator Huard. All his life he'd been trained and honed for one task—he and the others—and that task was to assassinate the hated despot. Chaos, his mentors had drilled into them, is to be preferred to ordered tyranny, to routine tortures, to the rape of entire worlds for the satisfaction of one man's twisted whim. If chaos must follow his rule, let there be chaos. But Huard hadn't given them a choice. He'd removed himself; and the training, the years, the education, and the indoctrination had been wasted. Nowhere to go, nothing to do, while everyone else greedily attempted to snatch up their portion of Huard's riches. Garbage pickers. He'd drifted, a trained killer, and eventually come here, a nowhere world, a world that could at least tolerate him if only because it didn't care. Young, sure of himself, proud, filled with unchanneled arrogance.

Arrogance like Aldhelm's. He reminded the Thane of his younger self. Aldhelm was not one of the original Hoorka, who had been little more than a motley set of criminals. Aldhelm had risen quickly and was still at the peak of his physical prowess.

Chaos *had* followed Huard, a long stretch of time in which worlds were sometimes out of touch with one another, sometimes forgotten, sometimes lost.

But the Alliance had come, loosely restructuring the order of human space, allowing variety but striving to retain order. Like all government, it worked—part of the time.

Sometimes the Thane thought of retiring, of passing on the figurative scepter, but there had always been one more thing to do, one more minor crisis to settle. Now there was a major conflict, and he was left with uncertainty and the onus of leadership.

He wanted it.

He didn't want it.

In time, he slept.

§　§　§

And the next morning . . .

"A new contract, Thane, with payment already enclosed."

"Who is it from?"

A rustle of parchment, the tearing of a seal.

"From the Li-Gallant Vingi."

"He is giving us another chance at Gunnar, then?"

Silence freighted with affirmation.

§　§　§

"The Hoorka-thane is here, m'Dame."

"Send him in."

The embassy worker turned from the desk holo and pointed to a door across the lobby. "Take that corridor, sir: third door on your left." He spoke without looking up from the microfiches on his desk. The Thane, his face set, turned and walked to the door without a word.

He found himself wondering why he'd come. The cool, impersonal efficiency of the Regency irritated him, and it took an effort to restrain himself from shouting and stalking out. He—his world, in fact—was not used to the cumbersome machinery in which a sophisticated society cocooned itself. They'd been too long isolated from the mainstream of human culture, and enough generations had passed for them to become used to a slower pace. Enough time had slipped by to find them filled with resentment tinged with envy at having to confront that sophistication again.

The Regent's office was not as the Thane had expected. The door dilated before he could knock. The room beyond was Spartan, not at all the ostentatious splendor he'd expected. There was an animo-painting covering one wall and a sculpture on the small desk behind which the Regent sat, motioning him in. She waved a hand at the only other piece of furniture in the room, an unpadded chair.

"Sit down, Thane."

He took the chair. The Regent folded her hands and rested her chin on them. "What can I do for you, Hoorka?" Her voice was as antiseptic as the room, but the Thane realized now, having seen her environment, that it was not haughtiness but simply her personal manner. The knowledge didn't relieve the tension.

"I assume you're aware that the Li-Gallant has renewed his contract for Gunnar."

A faint smile ghosted across the Regent's face. "So my sources tell me. I'm afraid Vingi is rather unimaginative."

"Gunnar hasn't the finances to void the contract."

"I also realize that. His is a movement growing in popularity, but poor. Does it bother the Hoorka that you are essentially working for the rich? It's a point of interest of me."

The Thane forced his face to show nothing. He replied in words as icily removed as the Regent's. "In our society, wealth is a sign of power. Those endowed with survival traits will survive, and money is one of those things that make survival easier. That's one answer. And remember that we will only attempt the assassination. Gunnar can—did—escape. That's also survival."

"It seems rather cruel, nonetheless."

The Thane stifled a retort, then spoke. "The 45th code line states that the Hoorka will not attempt more than two assassinations of any individual."

"Ah, a new rule."

"Yah, m'Dame. We've no intention of serving as a protective service for the rich, nor for the poor. We endeavor only to be fair."

The Regent shook her head. She used little fashionable attire, and only her earlobes were dashed with color—yellow green. "The Hoorka are interesting, if nothing else. I'll be honest with you, Thane. I don't think your people can do much offworld. I think you might be swamped with complexities once you set foot off a rural world. There are a thousand problems that arise, one of which is whether we want murder—and it is murder, however you dress it—sanctioned to walk the streets of other worlds. However, that's not a question for myself or the Alliance to decide. It would be up to the individual governments—and I have had inquiries.

"You'd have to be carefully policed, always under scrutiny to be certain of your fairness. Taint your organization at all, and you become little more than paid killers—and one can find them on any world. Shorn of your nice sophistries of survival and fate and chance, you are nothing."

She sat back in her chair, obviously waiting. The Thane knew she'd say nothing else and the irritation that he'd felt all along grew stronger. He railed at himself inwardly for coming here. He'd thought he could tell her of the problem Hoorka faced, make her aware of what Aldhelm felt and perhaps gain her support by being open, but no. She was already unsure of Hoorka and the admission of doubt in Hoorka's mind would spell their demise. No, he couldn't tell her.

"If Gunnar dies, what will that prove to you, m'Dame?" The control the Thane had been exercising faltered. He stood abruptly and strode to the wall where the animo-painting swirled. He stood there for a moment before turning to face her again.

"If he died, would that prove Hoorka's innocence? If he lives, does that prove guilt? I fail to see that, either way."

"If he dies, it seems to me that you have no ties with Gunnar. That seems obvious, Thane. And it would be quite a coincidence if he lives. Doesn't that make sense to you?" The Regent stared at him and they locked gazes for a moment. The Thane was first to look away.

"It is still possible that he could escape, and it would prove nothing. The victim always has his chance."

"Are you telling me he will get by you?"

"No." The Thane nearly shouted the word.

"That is good."

"M'Dame, all I wish to know is, if the Hoorka can prove innocence, will you give consideration to offworld contracts?"

"Thane, I promise you only that we'll be watching this carefully."

§   §   §

It was perhaps a measure of Gunnar's altruism that, when the contract was made public, he immediately sought refuge in solitude rather than remaining with his compatriots. Or perhaps they, his compatriots, fearing for their own lives, simply forced him to leave. Whatever the reasons, it made the job simpler for the Hoorka. They had had to storm citadels of resistance before, and it had always been costly in lives, even those of Hoorka-kin. So it was with a certain amount of relief that the Thane received the news that Gunnar had fled alone to the forested ridges of the mountains.

The report from the shadowing apprentices stated that Gunnar had carried with him neither weapons nor bodyshield. The Khaelian daggers were once again laid out for use by the Thane and Aldhelm—for the Thane had insisted that the rotation be changed for this one case. He was adamant. Hoorka would send their two best representatives.

It was a little past midnight when the Thane and Aldhelm caught up with the apprentices. One of the shadowers gave them a final report and traced on a map the trail Gunnar had taken and where he'd last been seen, a few kilometers away, by another apprentice, waiting up ahead.

The Thane shrugged his nightcloak over his shoulders and stared into the rustling darkness that flowed under the trees. A cry from some nocturnal animal shrilled nearby, and the stars touched the outline of the leaves. A moon was just rising above the slopes, but its light barely reached the clearing in which they stood.

"Let's go, then." The Thane turned to the apprentice. "We'll contact you if we need assistance with the body."

"Yah, Thane." The apprentice, in a shivering of darkness, left.

Without a backward glance at Aldhelm, the Thane half-ran into the forest, and after a moment, Aldhelm followed. Nothing had been decided. The conflict of the night before had never been resolved. The meeting had ended in uncertainty, and the Thane had found himself unable to make a decision about Aldhelm's suggestion. He knew that was a bad trait in a leader, and he knew that Aldhelm stood firm in his convictions. It might cause trouble. The spectre of fear chasing him, he ran.

They followed the trail blazed by the apprentices. It meandered up and down the rough slopes, but always led into the depths of the forest. It seemed obvious that Gunnar knew the area and had chosen his ground well. The cover was thick and abundant, and both Hoorka knew their quarry would be difficult to track down.

Nothing was said between them. They used their energy only for pursuit and left their thoughts unvoiced. The Thane was filled with apprehensions, wondering what Aldhelm would do, and wondering whether he could stop him or whether he even wanted to. For the first time he could remember, the situation seemed out of his control. He hated the feel-

162

ing, blamed himself for it. Aldhelm, when he glanced at him, seemed intent only on the hunt—if he harbored doubts, he kept them well hidden.

It was nearly three hours later when they came upon fresh signs of Gunnar—a trampled section of underbrush. There they met, then dismissed the last apprentice.

"Anything else we should be aware of?" The Thane and Aldhelm paused for a moment to catch their breaths.

The apprentice started to shake his head, then shrugged. "Not really, Thane. I once thought I saw something following me, a small globe, but it was gone before I could be certain. I was probably mistaken."

The Thane glanced at Aldhelm, but the Hoorka wasn't listening. The Thane felt his stomach knot. Hover-holos, he thought. That's what it could be. The Alliance could be watching.

Still he said nothing, and they went on, following the spoor of a desperate man: broken twigs, a fragment of cloth impaled on thorns, a muddy slope furrowed by hands grasping for holds. The forest began to thin, the trees spaced further apart, letting the moonlight dapple the ground. They crossed rock- and boulder-strewn fields carpeted with tall grass. Twice now, they had caught a glimpse of a figure far ahead, and each time it had disappeared. Gunnar was moving with confidence, so that the Hoorka remained a constant distance behind him, never closing the gap, never falling back. It was a situation that profited only Gunnar, for dawn was not far off. The Thane, angry and frustrated, cursed openly and exhorted Aldhelm to move faster. Their breath was ragged and loud, misting in the early morning coolness.

"Aldhelm, can you see him?"

"No, Thane."

"Damn." The Thane fingered the hilt of his dagger, stroking the well-used leather of the scabbard.

"He can't be too far ahead, Thane, and he has to

rest soon. He can't keep up this pace."

"Nor can we."

Aldhelm looked back over his shoulder, his eyes arcing flame. "We don't have a choice, Thane. If you can't keep up, I'll go on alone."

"Aldhelm."—wearily—"Remember the code. If he lives, he lives. It doesn't concern us."

"If he lives, we die." Each of the last two words was uttered in an explosion of breath, each syllable separated by silence. The grass beneath them rustled in the breeze with harsh whispers. "We've argued the point, but you can't deny I'm right, Thane. Gunnar has to die tonight, no matter how."

The Thane shook his head. "Not—"

"Yes!" Aldhelm cut in sharply. "You're growing soft. You're not looking at this realistically."

The Thane looked about them. No, he couldn't see any evidence of probing eyes, and no, there was no sign of Gunnar. "And if the Alliance is watching?"

"It's a chance we have to take, isn't it?" Aldhelm's voice softened, but his eyes were hard and unrelenting. "I've nothing but respect for you, Thane. Leave if you wish. But Gunnar dies."

"So we lose our integrity either way."

"Would you have integrity or survival? You said it the other night. The creation must transcend the creator. And his rules, in this instance."

"Or is it simply that you don't trust those guidelines? If so, it's you who are betraying Hoorka." The Thane scuffed his boots against the ground, and gravel rasped against leather.

Aldhelm, in answer, turned and strode away. The Thane looked at the ground, then at the dwindling back of Aldhelm, and slowly followed.

It was nearing dawn when they finally saw Gunnar, scrambling up a ridge above them, a deeper darkness etched against the satin sky. Either he couldn't see the assassins below him wrapped in their nightcloaks or he no longer cared, for though he glanced downward several times, he made no effort to seek cover. He fought his way upward and the stillness carried to the Hoorka the sound of dislodged pebbles falling.

"We have to get closer, Aldhelm. The daggers won't reach him."

Aldhelm made no reply. He stared at the figure above them as if the intensity of his gaze could halt the man's flight. Then he swept his nightcloak over one shoulder and drew an instrument from his shoulder pack. It glistened metallically in the moonlight. The Thane recognized it—a hand laser—and he knew the charade was over.

"Aldhelm, Gunnar has no bodyshield."

"I know it."

"The code—"

"Damn your code." He sighted down the barrel. Above them, Gunnar felt for a handhold.

"The Alliance, then! Think, man, they might be watching!"

"NO!" The words were a screech, a wail. Against the stars, Gunnar turned, startled.

"Aldhelm, the Regent will protect us if we follow the code. I feel that." The Thane knew he was trying to convince himself as much as Aldhelm.

"I can't believe you. I'm sorry, Thane." He held the laser in position, waiting.

And, at once . . .

Gunnar stood, a silhouette. Aldhelm's finger tightened on the trigger. The Thane loosed a dagger.

Aldhelm fell, his cry echoing among the peaks.

It was over.

§   §   §

Aldhelm awoke with the unsmiling face of the Thane hovering over him. Beyond the face he could see the fissured walls of Underasgard. He felt the coarse nap of a blanket against his skin, and to his ears came the faint sound of voices beyond the closed door of the chamber.

His face evidently showed his incredulity, for the Thane moved away and spoke: "That's right. You're back in the caverns, and still breathing."

With an effort, Aldhelm managed to struggle into a sitting position. His mouth was dry and stiff, and the words rasped and scraped their way from his throat.

"The contract?"

The Thane shrugged. "Gunnar lives."

"And the Li-Gallant?"

"Rather upset. But he can do nothing." The Thane found himself reluctant to talk about it. He wondered at himself, and forced himself to say more. "The Alliance had been watching, as I said. The Regent showed Vingi their record of the night, and that satisfied him, at least publicly." The Thane's gaze was like the sting of a weapon.

"I did what was best for Hoorka," Aldhelm said.

"Really?"

Before Aldhelm could reply, a young apprentice came in, the light of the main caverns behind her. She bent her head in salutation. "Thane Mondom has received a new contract. She'd like you to see it."

"I'll be there in a moment."

The apprentice bowed again and left.

Silence enveloped them. It seemed a long time before it was broken. "Thane Mondom?" Aldhelm's voice was a melding of melancholy and question.

"I dealt poorly with the last situation. If I'd been stronger, perhaps you wouldn't have gotten a dagger in you. And she is capable: perhaps not as good a knife-wielder as you, but she follows the code." The Thane shrugged.

Again, silence. There was nothing to say. After a moment, the Thane nodded to Aldhelm and left the chamber.

Outside, he leaned against the door as his thoughts lashed at him. To hear another called Thane had struck him more deeply than he wished to admit. At least he was still Hoorka, still of the kin.

He hoped it would be enough.

THROUGH TIME AND SPACE WITH FERDINAND FEGHOOT—TWICE!
by Grendel Briarton

Here is an entry in the IA'sf competition to determine, finally, if anyone can write worse puns than Dr. Asimov. Mr. Briarton is a member of the Oregon SF colony, having moved there from the San Francisco Bay area at the same time as his close associate, Reginald Bretnor, who is the editor of the unsurpassed symposium on writing SF: The Craft of Science Fiction

ON POACHING

"I'm so glad you've returned, Mr. Feghoot," said Queen Victoria, as they sipped Highland whiskey in her sitting room at Balmoral Castle. "We do have a *most* difficult problem."

"Och, aye," declared John Brown, her devoted Scottish gamekeeper and friend. "It's that domned poacher, ye ken."

"You mean you still haven't caught him?" asked Feghoot.

"Sir, the problem is we *have* caught him—that is, we ken weel who he is, and there's naught to be done about it. He's Sir Andrew MacHaggis, Lord Chief Justice of Scotland, and there's scarce a day when he doesn't shoot a good dozen of our cock pheasants. Then he hides the birrds in a hole in the wall, and comes here bold as brass to pay his reespects. He desairves to be shot, but ye canna shoot a Lord Chief Justice of Scotland."

"No," sighed the Queen. "Nor can we drag him to court like a common criminal. We must think of public opinion. Yet punished he must be. Oh, Mr Feghoot, what shall we do?"

Feghoot thought for a moment. Then, "Your Majesty," he announced, "I have a solution of which I'm sure Prince Albert would have approved. You can charge Sir Andrew quite properly with male pheasants in orifice."

ON PRAYING

Had it not been for Ferdinand Feghoot's quick thinking, Sir Richard Burton would never have become famous as the first Unbeliever to reach Mecca and his translation of the Arabian Nights never would have been published. Feghoot (who had made the trip many times over the centuries) kindly went with him, posing as a humble used-camel dealer.

As the caravan started out, the fierce desert sheik who was convoying it stared at Burton suspiciously. "Who is this man, Honest Akbar?" he demanded. "He doesn't look like a Moslem to me."

"He's a Pathan from faraway Hind," Feghoot told him. "That is why his appearance and accent are strange."

The sheik glared for a moment and galloped away and poor Burton sighed in relief. Then, at the midday halt, when they were all called to prayer, h made his mistake. He threw down his prayer rug, and prostrated himself—not to the East, like everyone else, *but to the West*.

Instantly the sheik and his men were upon him, their scimitars drawn, shrieking, "Slay him! Slay the uncircumcised infidel!"

"Stop!" shouted Ferdinand Feghoot in the nick of time. "O Sons of the Prophet, he didn't do it on purpose! He's just Occident prone!"

JOELLE
by Poul Anderson

*The author is a tall, wiry man with a
tendency to look shaggy even when walking
out of the barber-shop. He was born in
Pennsylvania, grew up in Minnesota and
Denmark, and now lives with his wife,
Karen, in Orinda, California (a place
which Robert A. Heinlein claims to be
a state of mind, which he believes in
the same way he believes in Oz). Mr.
Anderson's work ranges from rousing
rocket-&-graygun tales, like "Swordsman
of Lost Terra" from* Planet Stories, *through Limericks, Sherlockian
speculation, fantasy—and here, "Joelle."*

When the aircraft bearing him began its descent and he saw Lawrence, Eric Stranathan's first thought was: *But Joelle never said the place is beautiful!* He had imagined all Kansas to be like the plains that reached eastward and eastward of Calgary. Instead, a river gleamed between hills rich with trees while the town itself climbed from the water in streets and homes that had known the same shade for two and a half centuries, and the university campus might have been a huge park. After a moment he realized how little of anything she had ever told him about it . . . or about her entire life, but he knew the reason for that.

The aircraft dropped steeply, engines a-thunder. I was an American military jet, akin to those he glimpsed on patrol against summer-blue sky and summer-white cumulus clouds. Now he spied the base for which it was headed. That too was a surprise, as small as it appeared, a field and a few buildings, until he reflected that most of it must be underground, hardened against missile strikes. Well the border of the ·Holy Western Republic was less than 400 kilometers toward sunset, and although the Yanks had been at peace with their dissident brethren for two decades, still, three civil wars in a many generations left scars which would not heal soon and perhaps never completely.

Pulse riotous, his body shoved at the safety harness as if wanting to leap out and beat the flyer to earth. He forgot landscape and politics. Joelle was down there.

Air cushion met concrete, the craft slid to a halt tripods thudded into place, power cut off, silence rang. Eric fumbled at his harness. He had never flown in a fighting vehicle before. His service unit at home was simply the domestic police, Canada having a policy of not assigning much-needed specialists to soldiering, where their skills were mostly irrelevant Beside him, Major Goldfine, his single cabin companion on the flight from Calgary, reached over to help

Despite the importance of this mission, the American had chatted amiably en route, had actually scoffed a trifle at the elaborate preliminaries and precautions. "Shucks, the Holies are too worried about the Mexican Empire these days to want trouble with us. We aren't. And as for you Canucks, why, Dr. Stranathan, isn't your coming here part and parcel of our countries drawing together? My money says the North American Federation will exist inside another ten years."

Eric had grinned to himself at being called a Canuck—he was tall, rawboned, sandy-haired, his countenance craggy as ancestral Highlands—and tried to respond in the same fashion. But he kept falling silent; his mind was always slipping off to seek Joelle.

He rose, bade the crew goodbye, ritually patted the autopilot, and followed the major out the door, down an extruded ramp. The day was warm, sun-dazzled, eased by a breeze which seemed to carry a breath of hay scent from agridomains beyond this field and those walls. He hardly noticed. At a gap in a fence, she was waiting. Somehow he did not run; but each footfall beat through its shin to the knee.

Had she changed in fifteen months? She was not dressed quite as he had ever seen her before, in the severe business outfit of the conference, the casual shirt and pants of their mountain holiday, the flowing Antique Revival gown she had bought toward the end—getting advice from a couturier—to please him. Today the slenderness and the fullness of her were clad in a high-collared blue tunic, blue trousers, and buskins which suggested the basic uniform of the American military without having its dash.

As he approached, she lifted an arm in half a wave: no more.

A large blonde colonel and a small black civilian flanked her, two noncoms bearing sidearms behind them. The colonel stepped forward. "Dr. Stranathan?" she greeted with an efficient smile. "Welcome. I'm

Maria Lundgard, chief liaison officer with the Shannon Foundation." Handshake; polite words. "Allow me to introduce Dr. Mark Billings, the head of it. You know each other by reputation, of course." Handshake; polite words. "And you have already met Joelle Ky."

Handshake—As he took hers in his, there flitted across Eric's mind the idea that these names, together with Sam Goldfine's, expressed something of what had made this strange, wounded nation wherein he stood. For Joelle, little save strong cheekbones bespoke, in the blood, what history her surname remembered. The helmet of bobbed sable hair, big dark eyes, delicate nose and jaw, mouth a bit wider than it might have been, clear pale complexion, 175 centimeters of height, must have come from many elsewheres, England, France, Russia, Cuba, Dacotah, who could now tell? Who cared? Her hand was branding his with its coolness.

"How good to see you again," she said, as she might to any colleague. Or was her contralto still more withdrawn than that?

(A message from her in December had warned: "When you come—because you are going to, you are, if I have to call a one-girl strike to make them arrange it—be prepared for a most correct reception. At first, I mean. They will be around too, you know, all the pushy theys that infest this world like flies, officers, officials, I know not who or what more. We won't let them see what we share, will we? It's none of their damn business, it's our private miracle. Oh, no doubt they suspect. Maybe they know for sure. I wouldn't put it past them to have sicced their nasty little bugs on me 'way up in your country. But they won't dare let on—the atmosphere, the negotiations toward union must never ever be endangered by any friction that can be avoided, "Union" is as sacred a cow as people have yet seen, though I admit she is a very dear cow to me too—anyway, if we stay discreet, they can't so much as hint we need a chaperone, not even under the excuse of security. Have no fears, darling. No bugs can crawl into *my* section. I've seen to that, and I don't let up on it. Once we're alone, wow, will we be indiscreet! How can I wait till then? . . .")

She looked so grave. "I, I'm anxious to get busy with you," he ventured.

"Likewise is everybody here," Billings said. Eric released Joelle. "But you must be tired from your flight, Dr. Stranathan, and certainly you'll want to get properly settled in before starting on as demanding a project as this will be." The director chuckled. "I know better than to push my linkers. They push back, hard."

"I think we, he and I would be wise if we have a preliminary run-through as soon as possible," Joelle urged. Her tone stayed level.

"Tomorrow?" Eric asked.

"Already?" Lundgard replied, surprised. "Why, I was planning to have you shown around, the sights, you know, and I'm sure the place is full of persons who're eager to meet you."

"Yes, no doubt," Joelle said, oddly hesitant.

"Uh, if, uh, if nobody will feel it's rude of me," Eric blurted, "I disagree. You and I, Miz Ky, we'd do best to, uh, get each other thinking about specific dimensions of what we hope to do." *Why isn't she insisting?* stabbed within him.

"Well, we can talk about that on our way into town," Lundgard decided. "I have a car ready. Sergeant, bring along our guest's baggage. This way, please."

Eric maneuvered to walk beside Joelle. He bent his arm, wondering if she would take it. In Canada he had been astonished—angry, at first—to learn that that simple gesture was unknown to her, and touched at how eagerly she adopted it. Today she did not notice, or pretended not to.

She wasn't all aloof. On the ride into Lawrence, she joined somewhat in the conversation. The banalities she avoided—How had his trip been? How were things in Calgary?—but that had always been her way. Likewise, she had scant interest in politics, on which the rest of the party cautiously touched— Did Dr. Stranathan believe General McDonough might really allow a parliament to be elected in Canada? If so, might that prove an obstacle to union, Congress remaining such a cherished symbol in the States? However, since President Antonov appeared sure to be succeeded by his nephew when he died, which he would any day, and the nephew favored federation, might still another U. S. Constitution be decreed?

But when talk veered to technical subjects, she grew animated. The latest R & D toward improving migma fusion powerplants; cryobiological discoveries announced from an orbital lab maintained by the Iliadic League; design of a spaceship which would carry twice as many colonists as at present to Demeter through the star gate; a proposal for a message to which the Others must, oh, must at last respond—As the spirit danced forth in her darting smile and gestures, pouncing questions, a remembered manner of tossing her head, Eric let the wonder of being beside her overwhelm him.

Yet when the car stopped at the university faculty club, where he would lodge, she said merely, "I'll call you later, if I may, after you know what else you ought to do, and we'll make a date."

(A message from her in April had warned: "I suppose I have been less passionate in my communications lately. Poor dear, how your last letter struggled to tell me without telling any censors! As a matter of fact, I don't guess our mail is being read, though we'd better not count on that; it's possible to do without leaving traces I could detect through my special system, if they went to a lot of trouble. But about us. Maybe I'm just running out of love words, seeing they have to flow in the one direction only. Or maybe—well, more and more, you, your homeland, everything seems like a dream. Did it really happen? Could it ever have? Can it? I am in a new linkage these days, subnuclear physics, and can't say much about it because it's so shatteringly strange. But it fills me till I find myself wrapped up in it off work too, and suddenly realize I've not thought about you for hours. They have *got* to let you come here soon, soon!")

Eric shook her hand once more. "Indeed," he responded. "This evening, may I hope?"

They had been less formal when first they met.

The memory bank

The International Conference on Psychosynergistics was more than an important scientific event. It was a large political move. The Covenant of Lima had supposedly established a framework within which peace could grow after generations of upheaval. A sharing of knowledge that governments had long kept jealously secret was a commitment to try to make that supposition be true.

Thus the gathering was a profoundly symbolic act, a breaking of bread together. Ultimately, for most of those who took part, it became a communion. More than a few would afterward find their lives on quite unforeseen courses.

The world as a whole—Earth, the Iliadic states, other space colonies which retained allegiance to some mother country, the Lunar settlements, bases throughout the Solar System, the Demetrians at the far end of the star gate—sensed this, and tried to follow along wherever news outlets existed. That created a certain amount of nuisance, albeit in a worthy cause. Besides being constantly seized by journalists, delegates had to sit through interminable opening ceremonies. General McDonough himself welcomed them to Calgary—well, that was all right, he was short-spoken. But later in the evening Nikos Drosinis, not content to be introduced as a Grand Old Man, felt called upon to explain to the public, in his thick English, what the subject matter was. True, the average layman had become a scientific ignoramus. Still, wasn't popularization the job of those same journalists?

"—the human brain, and hence the entire nervous system, can be integrated with a computer of the proper design. We have long ago progressed beyond the 'wires in the head' stage. Electromagnetic induction suffices to make a linkage. The computer then supplies its vast capacity for storing and processing data, its capability of carrying out mathematico-logical operations in microseconds or less. The brain, though far slower, supplies creativity and flexibility; in effect, it continuously rewrites the program. Computers which can do this for themselves do exist, of course, but for most purposes they do not function nearly as well as a computer-operator linkage does, and we may never be able to improve them significantly. After all, the brain packs some ten to the twelfth cells into a mass of about a kilogram. Furthermore, linkage gives humans direct access to what they would otherwise know only indirectly.

"For present, practical purposes, its advantages are twofold. (A) As I remarked, programs can be altered on the spot, in the course of being carried out. Formerly it was necessary to run them through, painstakingly check their results, and then slowly rewrite them, with possibilities of error, and without any guarantee that the new versions would turn out to be what we most needed. Once linkers and their equipment come into everyday use, we will be free of that handicap. (B) By the very experience, as I have also suggested, the linker gains insights which he or she could have gotten in no other way, and hence becomes a more able scientist—including a better writer of programs—when working independently of the apparatus, too."

Good Lord! Eric thought. He shifted in his chair. His eyes took French leave of the stage and roved around the auditorium. A couple of hundred heads, several of which had fallen onto their owners' chests; the walls beyond, handsome maple paneling, proud standards displayed of the provincial regiments which had helped see Canada through the Troubles; a neighbor's jacket, slightly scratchy against his own bare arm (the man was pot-bellied and white-goateed but might be fascinating to talk to); a subtle sense of pressure in the nearness of the chap on his left (slight, dark, Hindu race but surely not from India's tragic barbarism—maybe the Himalayan Confederacy?); despite air conditioning, a subliminal smell of flesh. . . .

"Linkage has therefore advanced research considerably, in those areas fortunate enough to have escaped the worst ravages of chaos," Drosinos was droning. "It will accomplish unpredictably much more as it moves from its present, mainly pilot stage to a global industrial routine. I expect this to be principally through computation and, perhaps, ultra-delicate manipulation of specialized equipment—not through control of ordinary machines, for which we already have adequate systems, human *or* robotic.

"I have my doubts likewise about the artistic potentialities. A few interesting experiments have been conducted. However, they have not gone far. Besides computer time being badly needed elsewhere, it seems unlikely that artists of genius will have the patience, inclination, or innate talent to go through the long and rigorous training that would make linkers of them. Yet I hope a few of the papers at our conference will tell us more about this area. Linkers do report that their experience has a transcendental quality, and various of them have made amateur attempts to communicate this through poetry, music, or graphics. . . ."

Eric nodded. He had tried that himself, without success. Well, he was unfitted by heritage and probably heredity—younger son of one of the neo-baronial families which gave their parts of British Columbia law, order, and rough justice; his memories running to wild hunts across mountainsides and through ancient rainy forests, to patrols against bandits and occasional fights with them, to accompanying hoarse-voiced coarse-handed gentle-hearted fishermen along the wonder of the Inland Passage, to carefree tumbling of servant girls, to evenings when hearths roared with fire and squadron pipers skirled forth the Songs of Our Dead and he was reckoned old enough to get drunk with men; then the scholarship offered him when he was eighteen, to study at the Turing Institute and perhaps, if he did well, become a fellow of it; and accepting, because McDonough's peace had made feudalism obsolete throughout the country, and he was not interested in empty titles, and anyway, he was a younger son; and his amazed discovery that throughout centuries, the mathematical titans from Pythagoras to von Neumann and beyond had wrought glory—it struck more deeply into him than any falling in love had ever done—

Damnation, there *were* no words for being in linkage, and he had yet to encounter notes or images that carried the truth. Linked, he saw—no, not "saw"—maybe, "He was"—the whole of a problem— no, not "problem," that was too fragmentary a concept—"undertaking?"—"rise-toward-comprehension?"—he went outside of himself, outside of the world.

"We must mount programs for finding thousands of young persons who have the gift. We must persuade them that, while a career in psychosynergistics is demanding, it has its great rewards."

Even the elementary analyses on which he had trained had taken him into themselves. And when, the stern years behind him, he became worthy of the frontier questions, for which no programs could be devised until their very meanings had been explored—

"Already we become able, not simply to advance our technologies, but to improve the societies in which we live."

Take the credit tax matter, as the most dismal-seeming example. McDonough was pledged to work for an eventual restoration of civil government, though probably not till after his death. (So were his American counterparts. They might or might not be sincere. Eric believed McDonough was.) To that end, he wanted measures which would encourage private enterprise and discourage the growth of bureaucracy. At the same time, the state did need revenues. Well, instead of an income tax, with the power over the individual that that entailed, why not a tax on interest-bearing loans, whether they be to a householder who accepted charges so he could defer paying his hydrogen bill, or to a corporation financing an asteroid mine?

Why not? Okay, what would the likely effects be on the economy? Obviously, people would pay cash whenever they could. How might that affect companies which provided them with short-term credit, and the employees of those companies, and the merchants whom the employees patronized? The average person, having more money in his pocket in the absence of income tax, would find that his increased mortgage payments made no difference in his everyday life—or would he? With no more writeoffs, the giant combines, borrowing money on a giant scale, might actually carry a larger share of the burden than hitherto. How would that alter business and politics?

The questions went on and on. They had no single answers, for there was no single model. The problem was to construct as many different models as possible—they could be as elegant as Adam Smith's or as crude as Karl Marx's—and play the game out within each such universe, and test the respective scores against real data. But real data themselves are selected; a model is always implicit in any set of them. So the logic itself must likewise be analyzed.

Eric remembered how he groaned when the Institute got the job and asked him to join in. He had just come from working out (taking into account gravitation, electromagnetic fields, solar wind and solar evolution, dust and gas clouds, known stars in this region and their own projected fates, galactic orbit dependent on a million changing configurations elsewhere . . .) a tentative future history of the planets of his sun.

But having accepted, he found himself creating n-dimensional spaces, and time-variant curvatures for them, and tensors within, and functions and operators that nobody had ever imagined before; he made a conceptual cosmos, learned that it was wanting and annulled it, made another and another, until at last he saw what he had made and, behold, it was very good. Each time the numbers rushed through him to verify, and suddenly he knew how much reality he had embraced, it was an outbursting of revelation. The Christian hopes to be eternally in the presence of God, the Buddhist hopes to become one with the all in Nirvana, the linker hopes to achieve more than genius—is there a vast difference between them? Yes: the linker, in this life, does it.

In days, hours, fractional seconds. Afterward he or she cannot entirely comprehend what happened. The high moment of love also lies outside of time; but we understand it better, when at peace, than the linker understands what the linker has known.

Doubtless it's for the best that I have the primitive background I do, passed through Eric. *Too many of my fellows lose taste for the ordinary world. I haven't.*

"—often enough suggested that by way of psychosynergistics, we may become able to have discourse with the Others. Of them, we really know only that, once we had found the star gate in orbit, they let us use it, showing us the way through it to reach Demeter. Nothing else. Nothing else, in the century since then. The stupendous fact of their existence has inspired spiritual revolutions which helped bring on chaos. I cannot believe this was their wish. Rather, I would say that the knowledge of them aided mankind, throughout every grief and anger, not to release those powers which would kill the planet. Now, perhaps, we have completed a hard apprenticeship and are ready for the next stage. I dare trust that this meeting will bring us closer toward direct communication with the Others."

I wonder, Eric thought. *My guess is that they live their whole lives as I do only once in a while. Except they do it far more fully. That's my guess.*

Again his vision wandered. Hoy, quite a woman a dozen seats to his right! Why hadn't he noticed before? Tall, well-formed, dark-haired, face as finely and powerfully formed as the arch of a seagull's wings. . . . Who was she? What? Yank, to judge by the cut of her suit. She sat chin on fist, lost in her own wilderness as he had been in his.

"—during the years of secrecy, our American colleagues have made a tremendous advance. I wish to thank personally, and I am sure on behalf of everyone else present, thank the post-revolutionary United States government for its wise, altruistic decision to make at least the basic principles of this new technology public. Some of the most significant papers at our meeting will deal with aspects of it. Suffice it for me to say tonight that an extra dimension has been added to linkage, initially for military purposes, lately for pure research. In this holothetic system, as it is called, conceivably we begin to approach direct perception of the noumenon. No doubt that is too Faustian a statement, especially at our own eo-stage of investigation—"

The young woman had roused a bit. So probably the new specialty was hers. She listened for a while before returning to wherever she returned to.

—Afterward, as things broke up and the crowd moved out, Eric pushed his way through until he met her. Boldness had often gotten him what he wanted, and had never cost him more than he could afford. "Excuse me," he said, reading her badge, "Miz Ky."

"Sir?" Her eyes were neither timid nor inviting.

He had worked out his approach beforehand. It involved no lies, merely implications; it was fragile, but he shouldn't need it for more than an introduction. "My name's Stranathan, as you can see. I'm a plain, digital kind of linker, but certain of the work I've been involved in has brought me toward the fringe of holothetic concepts, and I was given to understand that that's your field."

"Yes."

"Well, uh, well," (if she isn't a servant girl but a lady, start out shy) "I would like to talk to an operator in it. I mean informally, no commitment to be precise, maybe getting a little subjective, do you follow me? Soon, before the conference hardens."

"Well—" She considered. It wasn't coquetry, it was straightforward thinking; yet her fingers had a darling way of touching her cheek. "Mmm, yes, that sounds reasonable."

"You might be interested to hear what we've been doing in Canada," he pursued. "We haven't gone as far as you, in some directions, that is, but I get the impression we've explored some others further."

She nodded. "I have the same impression." The crowd shoved and mumbled around them.

He put on the smile. "If I'm not being brash, would you like to come down to the bar with me and chat for a while?"

"I'm not accustomed to alcohol," she said calmly.

"Oh, well, a soft drink if you'd rather."

"I would. You suit yourself, though." Her gaze met his, and he thought he had never seen a more total honesty. "Yes, thank you, Dr. Stranathan, I've come to exchange information and this looks like a good beginning. Shall we?"

Present time

His room at the faculty club was sizeable, comfortably furnished, joined to a private bath, and equipped on his account with typer, computer terminal, data

screen and printout. On top of a small fridge were glasses, soda, and a liter of his favorite whisky. He stroked the bottle, touched by the gesture, until suddenly his throat clenched. Joelle must have told them the brand. It must have been her idea from the start. Then why had she herself, today, been so barren of welcome?

Striding to a window, he stared out. Open, it gave him a breeze gone cool, scented by newly cut grass, and a second-story view across lawns and buildings. Light streamed nearly level from the west, drenching leaves with gold and turning panes molten. A few students wandered along the paths, boys and girls brightly garbed, several couples hand in hand. The sky brimmed with quietness.

And this was her environment, these past three years, he thought. *Quite a change from the military reservation where she grew up. Or was it, really? She told me how her teachers, trainers, experimenters, at last her associates as she matured into her work and it into her—they were mostly research types, scientists, carrying out the project for its own sake, even if they were engaged by the armed forces, not terribly different from the professors here. And is she less walled off on campus, surrounded by town, with air and telecom access to almost anywhere anytime she chooses, than she was on a hundred fenced-in square kilometers in the Tennessee backwoods?*

The phone chimed. He stumbled and nearly fell in his haste to reach it and punch accept. And then it showed him Colonel Lundgard.

"Hello again," she said genially. "I hope you're settled in and getting rested."

"Uh, yes." He was startled to notice on a clock that he had arrived a couple of hours ago. More time than he knew had passed while he stood mind a-swirl. "Yes, they've given me a nice lodging."

"You're having dinner shortly with Dr. Billings, you recall," she said. "As for tomorrow, I've been making arrangements. Lots of people are eager to meet you. At ten, a preliminary tour of the university as a whole, ending in the office of Dr. Johns, the president, you know. He'll take you to a luncheon where a group of chosen faculty members will be. Afterward—"

A surge went through Eric. "Wait a minute," he snapped. "What about Miz Ky?"

Lundgard looked surprised. "I beg your pardon?"

"I—" He swallowed, mastered himself, and spoke fast. "Look, I appreciate your efforts, but I've come mainly to collaborate with her, and I am . . . am impatient to get going. I haven't heard from her yet. Better not make any commitments till I do."

"What?" Lundgard paused before frowning. "I daresay she'll be in her laboratory tomorrow afternoon, when Dr. Billings takes you through the Shannon Foundation facilities. You can discuss a work schedule then if you wish. First you do want to greet the, um, the leaders."

From a practical viewpoint she was right, Eric knew. In fact, he was stupid if he acted arrogant. He had his appointment not because he was the best linker in Canada—he was good, had contributed to the advancement of techniques as well as using them to solve problems, but he was no Tremblay or Vlasić—no, Joelle had pulled wires on his account, month after month; quite likely she had worn Billings down. Furthermore, he was supposed to bear international goodwill. He should if anything be a mite humble.

His shoulders stiffened till they hurt. *God damn it, I'm of the House of Stranathan, my father was Captain General of the Fraser Valley, we do not truckle!* Underneath, he recognized that it was his blood which would not let him wait a minute longer than he must to be alone with Joelle. Nevertheless, the principle was important, on behalf of his nation as well as family and pride. Wasn't it?

He picked his way carefully among words. "Yes, I see your point, Colonel. But please see mine. I can't talk sense until I have a rough idea of what's ahead in this job, what its shape will be, its dimensions. Before then, social noises are a waste of everybody's time, aren't they? Nobody but Miz Ky can properly explain. Linkage is not like anything else people do." He pushed his lips upward. "You must know that, if you've been a liaison with the Foundation. Linkers are all weird."

They did have a reputation for eccentricity, though it stemmed from a minority of them. Most tended to cover bashfulness or boredom when they were away from their machines with an ultra-conventional mode of life, and were not self-assertive. Daily details did not seem worth arguing about. Eric's background had left him a creature of the world who sometimes—he would recognize afterward—behaved pretty flamboyantly. But much would be forgiven him in Lawrence if, at first, the staff assumed he was only marginally human. The truth ought to dawn on them too slowly to make them feel they'd been hoodwinked.

Lundgard appeared to take his line. "Well, if you insist," she said after a moment. "I can't understand why Miz Ky didn't raise the issue while we were driving in."

Nor I. Was she too troubled? And by what? How should I know? When will I? "My fault, probably," Eric improvised. "She could've been waiting to hear what I wanted. And I was, uh, tired after my flight, too tired to think straight."

"Shall I call her?"

"No! —Sorry. Didn't mean to yell. We'd best settle this between us, she and I. I'll let you know as soon as possible. Do please convey my regrets—" Conversation eddied away in formulas. "So long."

When the screen blanked, Eric's hands began to shake. Sweat was prickling forth upon him. He tossed off a stiff shot and felt it burn out part of the tension.

Should I ring Joelle myself? No, she distinctly said she would. Why hasn't she, then? I don't understand her any longer. Did I ever?

Abruptly, violently, he twisted the information knob for her office and home numbers. At neither did he get a response. He imagined her walking alone by the river, as she had told him she often did, thinking about—what? He recorded a message to both places, the bare statement that he had kept tomorrow clear in order to consult with her and requested she call back. A minute after he was through, he could not recollect just what his phrasing had been.

The sun went under. It was time for his dinner with Billings. He changed into his reservist's uniform, acceptable everywhere and declarative of his citizenship. Having been shown around upon arrival, he readily found the designated place in the building.

That was a room broad and gracious, wood-paneled, French doors ajar to let in fresh air but a fire crackling on a stone hearth to ward off chill. Fluoros were set soft enough that a hint of flamelight and shadow-dance wove across walls. For an instant, Eric felt himself back in the hostel at Lake Louise, and stood blinded. But it was merely stubby, gray-polled, chocolate-colored Billings who rose to greet him.

"I'd rather have received you in my house," the director said. "I'm a widower, though, and no private party can afford competent servants these days." A flunky arrived in answer to a pushbutton. "What would you like for an apératif?"

Eric chose a margarita. He had heard of that concoction, Yank or Mex or whatever it was, but never met it. The sour-sweet-salt iciness was refreshing. Food would be served on a table at the far end of the chamber. Meanwhile he and Billings sat down in armchairs facing each other.

"Smoke?" The director offered a box of cigarettes.

"No, thanks," Eric declined. "Tobacco's too hard to come by where I live for most of us to form the habit."

"Best for your health, of course. Still, I look forward to the small luxuries as well as the major benefits that increased trade will bring—eventually union, don't you also hope?" Billings lit one. The smoke drifted harsh to Eric's nostrils, as if underlining what came next. "I've heard from Colonel Lundgard. Do you really feel you can't go through those motions tomorrow? Feathers will be ruffled."

Eric tautened anew. "I'm sorry," he clipped, "but that's the way it is."

Billings shrugged. "Well, I'll smooth 'em down for you. Won't be my first such job." Amiably: "You linkers are an independent breed, shall I say, no matter how conformist a mask many of you wear." He turned grave. "You may find yourself up against the same difficulty. Self-determination, intransigence . . . peculiarity . . . an order of magnitude above your own."

The cocktail, on top of what he had gulped in his quarters after a day of weariness and shocks, was making Eric's head buzz a little. He took a defiant swallow and said, "You refer to Joelle Ky, right?"

"Primarily, yes. Brilliant, but—"

"But nothing. We got, got so well acquainted in Canada that—" *Hold on. Don't blurt, you clotbrain!*

Billings regarded him measuringly. "You did?" he murmured. "Are you sure? For openers, what do you know of her background?"

She had given Eric a few stark paragraphs. He decided he might as well let Billings repeat the information, possibly adding more. If nothing else, that would gain him time in which to take hold of himself. "Not a lot," he said, and leaned back with an expectant expression.

Billings puffed hard on his cigarette. "She was born in western Pennsylvania," he began. "An aircraft, crashing down out of a dogfight, killed her family when she was two. A military orphanage took her in; well, most things were military at that period. Pretty soon, because both her parents had been applied mathematicians, a team from Project Ithaca came and tested her. She showed such natural aptitude that she, along with a number of similar kids, was whisked off to White Pine Reservation in Tennessee. That's where she spent the next twenty-one years."

He fell silent. Eric made a reinforcing noise.

Billings stirred. "Oh, they weren't unkindly treated, the children," he said. "It may have been preferable to growing up in a dormitory or a close-rationed civilian foster home. Each of them was adopted by a married couple within the project, whose material well-being the armed service saw to. The grounds were extensive, woodsy, pleasant. There were ample recreational facilities. The community, however isolated physically, was decent and lively, full of high-powered intellects. News came in on the screens and faxes, or via those who had occasion to make trips outside. And . . . what of the project itself? Even to a child, wasn't that worth sacrificing a lot of so-called normal living for? You're a linker, Dr. Stranathan. You can presumably answer that question better than I."

"You make me wonder if I can, sir," Eric said low.

"I can't myself, for certain. Linkage arrived too late in my life. My experiences with it have necessarily been limited. You, your generation, you started sufficiently young to develop those abilities much further. Now what of those who began earlier yet, virtually as infants?"

"Well, yes, what about them?" Eric attacked. "Joelle—oh, you must know we're on first-name terms—when we met, she was a stranger to a lot of things that the ordinary person, that I too take for granted. But she learned fast, and was delighted. Damnation, she's no machine! She's a woman!"

At once he cursed himself for what he might have revealed. However, Billings didn't notice, or pretended not to. "What you say is true of most of those I've encountered," the director replied. "By average standards, overly cerebral. Naïve about society. Timorous or standoffish, as the case may be, about forming close relationships. And yet not pathological, any more than an athlete is who's concentrated on his bodily development at the expense of cultural activities."

"So why d'you hint Joelle and I may find it hard working together?"

"She's not only spent her whole remembered life as a linker, she's been part of the evolution of holothetics from the outset. That was the purpose of Project Ithaca, after all. She still is. In fact, since it was declassified, since she moved from White Pine to Lawrence, progress has accelerated like a torch ship. Research is no longer held to narrowly practical ends, you see. Workers are free to explore an infinity. A great deal of what they learn is unforeseeable, comes as a stunning surprise. And Joelle Ky has been, is right in the middle of it."

"Sure. Why am I here, if not to learn enough from her that I can advise my government how best to join in with your outfit and— Whoa, you've got me doing it. Repeating what we both know."

Billings raised his brows. "Do we? You in particular. Oh, some basic theory, some diagrams and experimental data and whatnot, were presented at Calgary. Since then, you and your colleagues have been in touch with various of our folk, you've received books and journals and so forth. You have a general idea about holothetic linkage. But have you had a real chance to consider the implications?"

Eric blinked and sat straight. "Why, they're revolutionary, of course. Regardless, though, the system is a natural outgrowth of what had been going on before. Different in degree, but not in kind."

Memory flashed. She stood before him again, on stage in the auditorium in Calgary, looking so small and alone that he wanted to gallop his horse across the heads between them to reach her, and he heard her read her paper in a voice that was likewise lost:

"—while linkage to macroscopic machinery has not proven cost-effective, the case has turned out to be different for monitoring and controlling scientific experiments. For this it is inadequate to supply the operating brain with numbers such as voltmeter readings and nothing else. For example, a spectrum is best considered—rationally appreciated—when the operator sees it and, simultaneously, knows the exact wavelength and intensity of each line. Through appropriate hardware and software, this can now be done. Subjectively, it is like sensing the data directly, as if the nervous system had grown complete new input organs of unprecedented power and sensitivity.

"Workers elsewhere have experimented with that. The principal thing Project Ithaca did was to take the next step. What is the *meaning* of those data, those sensations?

"In everyday life, we do not apprehend the world as a jumble of raw impressions, but as an orderly structure. Yonder we do not see a splash of green and brown; we see a tree, of such-and-such a kind, at such-and-such a distance. Although it is done unconsciously, yes, instinctively, since animals do it too, nonetheless we may be said to build theories, models, of the world, within which our direct perceptions are made to make sense. Naturally, we modify these models when that seems reasonable. For instance we may decide that we are not really seeing a tree but a piece of camouflage. We may realize that we have misjudged its distance because the air is more clear or murky than we knew at first. Basically, however, through our models we comprehend and can act in an objective universe.

"Science has long been adding to our store of information and thus forcing us to change our model of the cosmos as a whole, until today this embraces billions of years and light-years, in which are galaxies, subatomic particles, a long evolution of life, and everything else that our ancestors never suspected. To most of us, this part of the Weltanschauung has admittedly been rather abstract, no matter how immediate the impact of the technologies it makes possible.

"In order to enhance laboratory capability, Project Ithaca began work on means to supply a linkage operator directly with theory as well as data. This was more than learning a subject, permanently or temporarily. Any operator has to do that, in order to think about a given task. And indeed, outstanding accomplishments came out of the Turing Institute here, pioneering ways for the linked computer to give its human partner the necessary knowledge. Project Ithaca greatly improved such systems, and its civilian successors continue to progress.

"That has had an unexpected result. Those operators whom Ithaca trained from childhood, linkers who today are adults advancing the art in their turn, are more and more getting into a mode that I must call intuitive. A baseball pitcher, an acrobat, or simply a person walking is constantly solving complex problems in physics with little or no conscious thought. The organism feels what is right to do. Analogously, we have for example reached the point of manipulating individual amino acids within protein molecules, using ions directed by force-fields, in a manner that perhaps only the Others could plan out step by step. Likewise for any number of undertakings. Direct perception through holothetics is leading to comprehension on a nonverbal level.

"This is doubly true because our theoretical knowledge is far from perfect. Very frequently these days, a holothete senses that things are not going as intended, that something is wrong with the model—and intuits what changes to make, what the real situation is, as we so often do in our ordinary lives. Later systematic study generally confirms the intuition.

"My colleagues will be discussing various aspects of holothetic linkage. This introductory sketch of mine—"

Eric dropped jarringly back to awareness. "I'm sorry, I didn't hear you," he said.

"It was a difference of degree once," Billings repeated. "It is becoming a difference of kind. If it hasn't already."

"Yes, I know the sensationalistic speculations. But I know Joelle too."

Billings sighed and smiled. "Ah, well, quite likely you do, better than I. Two young persons—Let's not argue. Do you care for another drink?"

Dinner was pleasant. The older man had a marvelous store of reminiscences, not confined to his professional career. He was in turn sharply interested in Eric's boyhood, the feudal society now vanishing, the personality types it brought forth. "In Mexico," he remarked, "the word is *macho*. You find exactly the same kind of man in the medieval Icelandic sagas. Seldom in nineteenth-century America; the frontier era was too brief for the armed roughneck to mature into the armed gentleman. I suspect you western Canadians drew on a remnant of English tradition among you."

Eric wasn't sure whether he was glad when his visit ended. He would be if his phone held a message from Joelle. If not— Corridor and staircase clattered to his speed.

A red light proclaimed a recording. Eric's finger jarred against the playback button. Her voice fell toneless: "Since you want it, let's meet at my lab tomorrow noon. I'll have sandwich makings and will have made sure we won't be interrupted. Sleep late in the morning. What we'll do won't be easy for either of us."

The memory bank

While the conference lasted, he squired her around Calgary. That held plenty of marvels for her, museums, live plays, a symphony orchestra, a ballet troupe, gourmet restaurants, little crannies of intimacy, or simply evenings of beer and bull with his local friends. She had had a small exposure to such things in White Pine, more in Lawrence, but Calgary was cosmopolitan. Besides, no one had taken her in hand before as he did. He wondered why, when she was so fair, but dared not crowd her with personal questions. She was too quick to retreat into noncommittal correctness. And maybe that *was* why.

Their relationship struck roots and sent forth buds. By the time the gathering adjourned, she had accepted his invitation to Lake Louise. He had the family connections to get them into that resort, she had no trouble extending her leave of absence, and they were both well supplied with money.

On a certain early morning there, he knocked on her door. By then they had tramped the trails, scrambled onto the peaks, loafed in alpine meadows while birds and deer and once a bear went by. Today they would give to the lake itself. After breakfast he led her to a hired canoe. In the hours that followed,

197

sometimes they paddled, sometimes they used a whispery electric motor, sometimes they grounded the craft and went ashore. Whenever they sat on sun-spattered brown duff and wavelets glittered before them, he kissed her. She had first let him do that on one of their last outings in town. He would never forget lamplight splintered by June leaves in the park where they were, a sound of crickets, and her dear awkwardness. She learned fast and grew braver. Today his hand lay rounded inside her shirt, though that was where she stopped it. How lithe she was, how warm her odor. She murmured.

Between two such halts they shipped their paddles and idled. The water danced blue, green, diamond. Around it, above forest, mountains sheered aloft into silence. Ever so slightly, the canoe rocked with each motion they made.

She dipped a finger over the side and watched how ripples spread. "Electron interferences make a moiré too," she mused. "It's wonderful finding the same here. I never noticed before." Her glance captured him. "Thank you for bringing me." The eyes drifted elsewhere. "Electrons do it in three dimensions. No, four, but I haven't perceived that . . . yet."

He recalled similar remarks of hers. Over coffee and brandy afterward, she had told him how sublimely Newtonian *Swan Lake* and *Ondine* were, when to him they were sublimely sexy. Well, that could be innocence speaking; and he, a linker likewise, found as much mathematics as melody in a Bach recital, or admired above everything else the subtle perspectives in Monet. (Looking at the same 3-faxes, she had pointed out interactions of colors to which he and, he suspected, critics of the past couple of centuries had been blind) Today, for whatever reason, unease roused in him.

"Look, Joelle," he said, "Don't get lost in abstractions— Wait. Please. Let me explain what I mean. Sure, you and I work with data, set up paradigms, compute resultants, sure. Fine. Fine job. But let's not let that interfere with what we, well, we find in places like this. In our private lives generally. This—" he waved a hand around the horizon— "is what's real. Everything else we infer. This is what we're alive in."

She regarded him for a long while, during which he glowed. Finally her gaze moved away, once more outward. He could barely hear her: "I never got a chance to appreciate that before now."

"Jesus Christ!" broke from the quick pain in him. "What kind of monsters were they? Locking you away since you were a baby, treating you like a piece of apparatus. That's what you were to them, nothing but apparatus."

She shook her head, still staring from him. "No, Eric, I've told you that isn't true. Weren't you listening? The secrecy, the work itself, those were military necessities. My foster parents were as kind as ever my own could have been. They tried to get me to lead a normal life. I had plenty of age mates, children of personnel. But I found too much in the computers. Remember, holothetics wasn't something cut and dried that a school fed to me. It was something that grew, it was discovery, accomplishment, adventure, and from the beginning, *I* was a leader. That's a heady brew for anyone, let alone a kid. My contemporaries bored me, I discouraged every effort at friendship, except with the few who were in my part of the project, and we hardly ever wanted to do more than talk about it when we couldn't actually be in it. So, my fault entirely, I didn't appreciate that there are equally grand things, till I moved to Lawrence and suffered a healthy culture shock. And at first that drove me still further into myself."

She faced him afresh. "You've made the difference, Eric. You've made me feel and understand . . ." Her words trailed off. She flushed from temples to bosom.

"I'm glad," he said, and, to cover the confusion in them both: "Shall we push on?"

After supper cooked over a resin-fragrant fire and

seasoned by her nearness, they turned back. Sunset caught them, but they had foreseen that and the sky gave ample light. A kilometer or two from the lodge, they took a rest. Pinewoods hid it; they might have been the last man and woman on Earth, or the first on a virgin world. The lake glimmered like obsidian and, under a breeze whose chill Eric didn't notice, swayed the canoe on chuckling waves. The mountains seemed far off and airy, something dreamed long ago in a dawntide sleep. Stars crowded heaven, the Milky Way swung frost-bright among them, the sense of being afloat in measureless immensities could not have been greater were he spaceborne.

Vision ranging upward, she whispered, "How do the Others see that? What is it to them?"

"What are they?" he answered. "Animals evolved beyond us; machines that think; angels dwelling by the throne of God; beings, or a being, of a kind we've never imagined and never can; or what? Humans have been wondering for more than a hundred years now."

"We'll come to know." Her pride sounded forlorn.

"Through holothetics?"

"Maybe. Else through— Who can tell? But I do believe we will. I have to believe that."

"We might not want to. I've got an idea we'd never be the same again, and that price might be too high."

She shivered. "You mean we'd forsake all we have here?"

"And all we are. Yes, it's possible. And I wouldn't, myself. I'm so happy where I am, this moment."

She was silent for several heartbeats. "I am too, Eric. With you—" She moved toward him. The canoe lurched.

"Careful," he laughed automatically. "Yon water's mighty cold."

"Eric, let's hurry on." Her voice trembled with its own courage. "Start the motor. Bring us ashore where we belong."

Having landed, they stayed outside for another

hour, in which the mountains danced and the stars rejoiced, before they sought his room.

Present time

The Shannon Foundation was located on campus. As the single holothete to join it thus far, Joelle rated a building to herself, just adequate to contain the equipment she needed and an office, but electronically woven into a network which was becoming global. It stood between ancient oaks, whose leaves rustled to a wind that drove clouds and their shadows before it. Sleek plasticrete walls, pastel tinted, didn't fit into the surrounding greenery, the downhill riverward view of an old town and a gentle hinterland. *As if this were a shell shutting out the living world and me,* Eric thought. He activated the chime with his hand and knocked with his heart.

The door opened for him. There she stood. Her slimness was muffled in a coverall, the long black hair drawn into a ponytail, her eyes enormous.

"Oh, Joelle, Joelle!" He almost bowled her over, bearing her before him in his rush to let the door close them off while he embraced her.

She kissed him back, her touch also roved, and minutes passed that nobody counted. Yet when they stepped apart, fingers entwined, to see each other, she was not laughing or weeping and her breath came evenly. His did not, and it was through a faint blur of tears that he saw how seriously—compassionately?—she looked upon him.

He had spent much time composing what he would say, but it fled from him and he could only stammer, "How I've missed you. Never any more."

"If that's what you want, darling," she responded.

"Would you believe I've been chaste these fifteen mortal months? Silly, no doubt, but it was a thing I could do for you, it was a way of telling myself we would be together."

Her gravity yielded to a sunrise of blood such as he remembered from their earliest days as one. "Silly,

201

yes, and sweet and knight-erranty and what I'd have expected of you, Eric." Why did she appear unsure of herself?

"Well?" he called through the roaring within him.

She gathered a smile. "I expected that too. Come along."

There was a couch in her office, for occasions when she did not want to interrupt an endeavor to seek an apartment that her letters had described as cramped and lonesome. He slid the coverall off her with reverence, for she rose out of it like Aphrodite from the sea and made the drab enclosure shine. He was clumsy in removing his clothes, since he could not watch what he did.

At Lake Louise she had offered him her maidenhead, but she had soon learned how to give joy and take it as well as any woman he had ever known, except that being Joelle she gave him what went beyond joy. On this day—It happened fast in his eagerness, but she guided him with her motion and a few words, so that the billow crested in her before him. Afterward she lay quietly. Nor had she cried that she loved him, as he did to her.

The narrowness of the couch made it a rather ludicrous effort not to fall off, though it did bring him pressing up against her while he crooned nonsense. Still she rested passive, until at length she stirred and said, "No, dear, please, not again right away. We've got too much else ahead of us."

His fears stabbed him anew. He sat up, swung feet to floor, twisted around and confronted her. "What's the matter?" he demanded.

"Why, nothing . . . maybe. Everything depends on you, what you decide is best." She raised herself and reached forth to stroke his brow and cheek. Trouble crossed her face, as lightly as a cloud shadow on the grass outside. "A lot has changed while we were apart. Especially in the last few months." It passed as swiftly.

He grabbed her shoulders. Barely he kept his grip

from closing with bruising force, and felt instead how silken was the skin beneath it. "You've met somebody else?" he half shouted.

"No, no." She shook her head. He saw the ponytail swirl across her back, ebony on ivory. "Never, Eric."

"You've fallen out of love, is that it?"

"No. You'll always be *you* to me. But—" She sighed and slumped. "Other things have changed, yes. I couldn't help it, I might have quit if I'd foreseen, but the newness came sneaking in—or came like a blast of trumpets, oh, I don't know—" She straightened, locked her vision into his, and spoke with regained steadiness. "When you understand, and that's what I hope to make you do, when you understand, you can choose for us. I'll be glad to go along. I do love you." She uttered a laugh. "Sweetheart, this kennel includes a bathroom. Let's wash and get dressed and have a bit of lunch, and afterward we'll talk about us."

She's being as kind as she's able. The knowledge rocked him.

In the shower she, who had never been mercurial before, was suddenly playful, giggly as a schoolgirl. "Bodies are fun, aren't they? Mostly I've geen giving mine plain maintenance, because my work wanted fifty hours a day and anyway you weren't around. . . . No, Eric, darling, wait, we must get serious, both of us—" *I can't follow her mind, her feelings any longer, she's become a stranger. Or was she always? But what a bonny stranger. If we have to start over from zero, okay, I'm willing.*

Back in the office, she produced bread, cheese, sausage, beer from a minifridge and made sandwiches for them while she chattered. He did his best to reciprocate. They gossiped about colleagues, they swapped recollections, and finally they reached the subject of what they had individually been doing in the past months. Communications between them had been scanted of late. She had pleaded extreme busyness to account for the brevity and impersonality of hers and he, puzzled, failing not to be hurt, confined in any event to sending her nothing that third parties shouldn't know about, had cut his own letters short. They talked at intervals by phone, of course, and her image remained with him for days afterward exactly as it had appeared on the screen; but those calls could show no more than affinity sprung from a shared profession.

He told her about his latest assignment, a sequel to the work on economics, this an attempt to quantify political consequences of various strictly defined types. She nodded. "Yes, I see how that'd be quite a challenge," she said. "A bare preliminary, as you admit, a grotesque oversimplification, but . . . a beginning? If ever we do get a genuine theory of human interaction, parameters we can give values to, who knows? We might become able to abolish war, tyranny, poverty the way we've abolished cancer and schizophrenia."

He could hear she was being considerate of him, faking an interest she scarcely felt. Trying to awaken some enthusiasm they might share, he asked, "Do you think holothetics will help?" and laid his hand across hers where it rested on the desk.

She pondered for seconds. "Who can tell? But I doubt it. You see, it's a paradox, but in dealing with those social affairs, you're necessarily using an abstract, mathematical model. That isn't what holothetics is concerned with."

"No? Never, in all time to come?"

"What would the appropriate inputs be, ever?"

"The right model—"

Joelle braced herself. "Eric, in the past half year I've been discovering things about reality that make me see how jerry-built the whole idea of 'models' is that my science itself was founded on." She spoke fast, looking squarely ahead of her though he sat by her side. "I haven't told you, and I've scarcely hinted at it to Mark Billings, because—because I didn't realize either until very lately, what it signified that

I'd been experiencing." She turned around in her chair, toward him. Her free hand dropped to his arm. "I've spent the last few weeks trying to figure out how to explain to you, how to show you. I've been in touch with my associates from White Pine—we keep each other's secrets—and thought and thought about the results of experiments we've done involving regular-type linkers like you, and I personally—" She flushed anew. "I've only attempted full rapport with women. I wouldn't go that deep with any male except you."

She paused. "No, I lied there," she admitted. "I've not spent my whole time that way. Not when everything else has been opening up for me. But I've tried my damnedest, because I do love you, Eric."

In a rush: "Are you ready?"

"Yes," he made himself reply; for he more than half dreaded what lay in the inner building.

She leaned over and kissed him, lingeringly but altogether tenderly, almost as if she bade goodbye to a child. Then rising, she exclaimed, "Let's go!" and strode before him like the Victory of Samothrace.

The memory bank

After the mountains, they had a few days more in Calgary before she went home. On the second of these, a supper turned into a scheming session.

"Why must you leave?" he pleaded for the xth time. "You know you can have your pick of positions in Canada."

"But I can't," she replied softly. "You've no holothetic system in the country, and won't for years."

Bitterness coursed through him. "Yes, your career."

He saw her wince, and damned his tongue. A violinist was playing Mendelssohn's Concerto Number One; the notes flowed wistful around them. They had this part of the restaurant to themselves, their table by a window overlooking a lawn, rosebeds, and the

Bow River agleam in blue dusk. Candlelight glowed on her shoulders and arms, brought forth seductive shadows in the gown she had bought with such pride to make a show worthy of a Stranathan's woman, and sparkled off tears caught in her lashes.

"My life, Eric," she said. "You could give up linking if you had to, go back to the Fraser Valley, be a rancher, and not feel existence was drained dry. But you wouldn't willingly, would you? And you had those woods as a boy; it's in you to range them. I've only had my computers. Without them, I'd soon be nothing—have nothing to give you."

"I'm sorry." He reached across linen and crystal. "You're right, I'm wrong, it's only that it hurts too hard losing you."

"Not forever, darling. If we use the proper strategy."

They had talked about the matter before, but desultorily, soon veering away from a question that broke into their delight. Now he nodded. "We'd better work out a plan, then."

"The basic idea's simple. We wangle you an appointment to the Shannon Foundation."

"Couldn't I easier and quicker come down to the States and take whatever job is available?"

"No, I'm afraid not. The market is fairly well filled. Certainly you couldn't find a post in Lawrence or anywhere near. Besides, I'll be frank, the U.S. government is chary about admitting foreigners. Paranoid, if you wish, but don't forget what it's been through, these past decades. It'll ease up in due course, starting with Canadians. But meanwhile—in spite of the gesture made at our conference, and believe me, that was a huge gesture, we're saddled with a lot of official nosiness and suspiciousness."

"As your husband—I do want to marry you, Joelle—"

"And I you. Oh, I want!" Their hands clung. "But no. Not till the security regulations change. As they are, I'd be automatically excluded from defense-related research, and that's still a big part of what we do at Shannon. So I'd lose the very leverage I need to get you an appointment, where you too can have satisfying, meaningful work. Plenty bad I've prolonged my leave of absence. I dare not stretch it out."

"Can you, uh, spend your vacations here?"

"I won't have any for another year. And by that time, if everything has gone well, we'll be close enough to squiffling you into the Foundation that our best bet will be for me to hang in there and make sure of it."

"A year or worse! And I can't write or phone to say I love you, can I?"

"No, that'd be unwise. If they learn I'm 'emotionally compromised,' some bureaucrat is bound to take the safest course and deny you entry, as well as lifting my clearance." Joelle chuckled. The gallantry of that tore at him. "Once you're established among us, a romance leading to a marriage will be perfectly natural and cause no trouble." Her humor faded. "You're right, though. Those will be dead months, waiting for you."

"We can maintain professional contact," he said. "In fact, we must, to make it plausible that you push my candidacy. Let's have a few code phrases. 'Erratic feedback' means 'I'm off my orbit for lack of you.' 'Hyperspatial configuration' means 'You're a walking miracle.'"

"And you, Eric. . . . Hold on. I can improve on that. I can write to you, whatever I please."

"Huh?"

"Yes." Excitement animated her. "Data systems in the two countries will shortly be interconnected, you remember. I can input information without its registering on any monitor. You can't, but I can, and route it to your private terminal. The holothetic system enables me. In effect, I take over a whole channel, including its registers and memory."

He whistled at the magnitude of that capability.

"Ah, ha, I've surprised you," she laughed. "Well, a girl ought to surprise her man once in a while, true? Wait till you see my letters. They're going to be so erotic the printout will smoke."

"I'll kiss it just the same," he said.

"Never expected I'd want to be a printout. . . ." She grew solemn. "Eric, can you imagine what you are to me? What you've given me? The whole material universe, that's what, from that garden out there that I now fully see and feel and smell—" she gestured at it; darkness was rising swiftly from the earth, but the earliest stars were kindling overhead— "and this nice tickly champagne in my mouth, on from those to the novas exploding when you make love to me—and then to top the treasure off, *yourself*, body, mind, soul, your funny lopsided smile and your recollections of home and the countless courtesies you don't even notice you're doing me—" Joelle covered her eyes. "Pardon me if I blubber for a minute. It's not from being sad. I am that, sure, but only on th-th-the surface. Underneath, where it counts, I'm aleph-sub-aleph happy."

Present time

The hardware filled a large bleak room, and at that much of it was below the floor in a cryogenic chamber. Principally Eric saw four metal cabinets, taller than himself and thrice as long, standing parallel to each other. Instruments, displays, and controls upon them were for the benefit of service technicians; once linked, the woman had no need of such gadgets. Behind them he recognized the bulk of a Heydt 707, similar to the machine with which he worked at the Turing Institute and, she had informed him in their "public" communication, lately modified and reprogrammed for his benefit. In front of the apparatus were four equally familiar loungers and their attached linkmakers. He knew that sometimes she teamed with up to three visiting holothetes, as well as employing ordinary operators like himself for assistants.

208

Today, they two were alone. Windowless, the room was fluorolit, a whiteness that felt cold though ventilators hummed forth warm currents of air. Silence pressed inward. He looked at her and thought, *But for me, she might never have known anything more than this; sun, stars, wind, leaves, flowers, heights, every joy there is would be ghosts she hardly noticed, and love would not exist.* Yet the distress he had sensed in her earlier was gone. She stood before her machines and fairly blazed with ardor. For a skipped pulse he wondered if she had forgotten him.

But she spoke, rather quickly, not facing him: "You caught me off guard, dear. I assumed you'd spend your first few days being sociable as you were supposed to. I should have recalled you don't brook being told what to do. I figured I'd plan this demonstration according to how you seemed to react, to feel—fifteen months is a long time apart, you might have changed, in any case we haven't had years to get acquainted. Well, I'll have to improvise. Forgive me if it comes heavier than I hoped for you."

"What are you talking about?" he asked, seizing her elbow the way that fear seized him.

She turned and considered him steadily, her countenance gone strange, before she replied, "Words are no use here. You must experience for yourself. We're about to become more intimate than ever in bed. Enormously more."

Quasi-telepathic effects had been reported, when a passive linker in a holothetic circuit not only received the same data in his brain as the active one did, but "felt" the latter's ongoing evaluations. "You, uh, you'll slave my unit to yours?" Eric inquired. "According to what I've seen in the literature, that doesn't convey a particularly strong or clear perception."

"Everything isn't in the literature yet. I told you I—we—all right, I am making whirlwind progress. I've acquired a, I don't know, an insight, a near-instinct, and the feedback between me and the system, the continuous reprogramming at each

209

session—" She tugged his sleeve. "Come along. Get to know!"

"What do you have in mind?"

She frowned the least bit. "That'll depend partly on you, how you're taking what happens. We'll begin with you and the 707. Just think in it for a while, get settled down. Then, through the cross-connections, I'll phase you in with me and my computer. That will have to be strictly input to you, no access to effectors, or you might ruin some delicate experiments. I'm going to look in on them, you see. My help is called for often enough that we have constantly open channels between them and my system. Genetics at a lab right on this campus; nuclear physics at the big accelerator in Minnesota; cosmology in Sagan Orbital. I hope I can lead you to a hint of what I'm doing these days. I'll know, because you will have an output of a kind to me. In effect, I'll be scanning your mind. Yes," she said into his stupefaction, "I've reached that stage.

"Afterward—" She threw her arms around him and kissed him. "Let there be an afterward."

He responded, but couldn't help thinking that her tone had been kind rather than prayerful. *Well, why should she fear? Isn't her work going well, and aren't we together again?*

He lowered himself into the proper lounger, adjusted it to the reclining angle he liked, let muscle and bone ease into its form-fitting comfort until he felt almost disembodied, before he pulled the helmet down over his head, adjusted and secured it, put his wrists through the contact loops, tapped fingers across a control plate and checked out the settings. A side glance revealed Joelle doing likewise in a rig that appeared little different from his. And the olden thrill shook all fret out of him. Once more he was going to become transhuman.

"Activate?" he asked.

"Proceed," she answered.

"I love you," he said, and pressed the main switch.

Momentarily, senses and consciousness whirled, he imagined he heard a wild high piping, memories broke forth out of long burial as if he had fallen back through time to this boyhood swimming hole and moss cold and green upon a rock, that hawk at hover and the rough wool of a mackinaw around him. Then his nervous system steadied into adjustment, into mastery. Electromagnetic induction, amplification of the faintest impulses, a basic program which he had over the years refined to fit his unique self, meshed; human and computer became a whole.

"Think," she said. How could he not, when his was now a mightier intellect than any which had been on Earth before his day?

"Words are no use here," she said. Never would they tell an outsider the least part of that which dwelt in him.

He was fully aware of his environment. Had he wanted to, he could have examined its most micrometric details, a scratch and a reflection on polished metal, the shimmy of a needle on a meter, mumble and faint tang of oil in the ventilation, back-and-forth tides in his veins. But they didn't matter. Joelle herself no longer was quite real. He had a conceptual universe to conquer.

In the next several milliseconds, while he cast about for a problem worth tackling, a minor compartment of him calculated the value of an elliptic integral to a thousand decimal places. It was a pleasant, semi-automatic exercise. The numbers fell together most satisfyingly, like bricks beneath the hands of a mason. *Ah,* came to him, *yes, the stability of Red Spot vortices on planets like Jupiter, yes, I did hear talk about that in Calgary.* The sweep hand on a wall clock had barely stirred.

He marshalled a list of the data he thought he would need and sent a command. To him it felt much like searching his normal memory for a fact or two, except that this went meteorically faster and more assuredly, in spite of drawing on memory banks which were hundreds of kilometers away. The theory reached him, equations, parameters and their specific values for Jupiter, yes, that particular differential equation would be an absolute bitch to solve except that he saw a dodge; but wait, was it actually plausible, couldn't he devise a set of relationships that better described conditions on an aborted sun—?

An ice-clean fire arose, he was losing himself in it, he was getting drunk on sanity.

Eric: no voice, no name, a touch; Joelle.

He must wrench his attention from Jupiter, with a vow, *I'll be back*. Probably he would not have done it for anyone but her. He was no less a human male than when unlinked, he was simply a mathematico-logical super-genius. Though also, this time—Lying back, eyes closed, he caught what might be the first gleam of a revelation.

Eric, are you ready to follow me?

It was not truly a question, it was an intent which he felt. It was her. At dazzling speeds, as neurone webs adapted to each other's synapse patterns, she merged with him. The formless eddies that go behind shut lids were not shaping into her image; rather he got fleeting impressions of himself, before her presence flooded him. Was it her femaleness he knew as a secret current in the blood, a waiting to receive and afterward cherish and finally give, a bidding she chose not to heed but which would always be there? He couldn't tell, he might never know, for the union was only partial. He had not learned how to accept and understand most of the signals that entered him, and there were many more which his body never would be able to receive. That became a pain in him as it was in her.

Eric, in this too you are my first man, and I think my last.

Forebrains, more alike than the rest of their organisms, meshed. Besides, Joelle had practiced cross-exchange on that level and developed the technique of it with fellow linkers, until she was expert. Communication between her and Eric strengthened and clarified, second by second. It was not direct, but through their computers, whose translations were inevitably imperfect. Impressions were often fragmentary and distorted, or outright gibberish—bursts of random numbers, shapes, lightflashes, noises, less recognizable non-symbols, which would have been nightmarish save for the underlying constancy of herself. What touched his mind as her thoughts were surely reconstructions, by his augmented logical powers, of what it supposed she might be thinking at a given instant. The real words that passed between them went in the common mortal fashion, from lips to ear.

Nevertheless: he took her meanings with a fullness, a depth he had not dreamed could be, there on the threshold of her private universe.

"Genetics," she said aloud. That was the sole clue he needed. She would guide him to the research at this school. Knowledge sprang forth. The work was on the submolecular level, the very bases of animate being. She was frequently called on to carry out the most exacting tasks, invent new ones, or interpret results. Today the setup was in part running automatically, in part on standby; but she had access to it anytime.

Her brain ordered the appropriate circuits closed, and she was joined to the complex of instruments, sensors, effectors, and to the entire comprehension man had of the chemistry of life. Receiving from her, Eric perceived.

He got no presentation of quantities, readings on gauges whose significance became clear after long calculation. That is, the numbers were present, but in the experience he was hardly more conscious of them than he was of his skeleton. He was not looking from outside and making inferences, he was *there*.

It was seeing, feeling, hearing, traveling, though not any of those things, for it went beyond what the poor limited human creature could ever sense or do,

and beyond and beyond.

The cell lived. Pulsations crossed its membrane like colors, the cell was a globe of rainbow, throbbing to the intricate fluid flow that cradled it in deliciousness, avidly drinking energies which cataracted toward it down ever-changing gradients. Green distances reached to golden infinity. Beneath every ongoing fulfillment dwelt peace. The cosmos of the cell was a Nirvana that danced.

Now inward, through the rainbows, to the interior ocean. Here went a maelstrom of . . . tastes . . . and here reigned a gigantic underlying purposefulness; within the cell, work forever went on, driven by a law so all-encompassing that it might have been God the Captain. Organelles drifted by, seeming to sing while they wove together chemical scraps to make stuff that came alive. As the scale of his cognition grew finer, Eric saw them spread out into Gothic soarings, full of mysteries and music. Ahead of him, the nucleus waxed from an island of molecular forests to a galaxy of constellated atoms whose force-fields shone like wind-blown star-clouds.

He entered it, he swept up a double helix, tier after tier of awesome and wholly harmonious labyrinths, he was with Joelle when she evoked fire and reshaped a part of the temple, which was not less beautiful thereafter, he shared her pride and her humility, here at the heart of life.

Her voice came far-off and enigmatic, heard through dream: "Follow me on." He swept out of the cell, through space and through time, at light-speed across unseen prairies, into the storms that raged down a great particle accelerator. He became one with them, he shouted in their own headlong fervor, the same speed filled him and he lanced toward the goal as if to meet a lover.

This world outranged the material. He transcended the comet which meson he had become, for he was also a wave intermingling with a trillion other waves, like a crest that had crossed a sea to rise and break at last in sunlit foam and a roar—though these waves were boundlessly more shapeful and fleetly changeable, they flowed together to create a unity which flamed and thundered around an implacable serenity—*Bach could tell a little of this,* passed through him, for he had his reasoning mind too; that was a high part of the glory—*but he alone could, and it would only be a little—*

The atom awaited him. Its kernel, where energies querned, was majestic beyond any telling. Electron shells, elfinly a-sparkle, veiled it from him. He plunged through, the forces gave him uncountable caresses, the kernel shone clear, itself an entire creation, he pierced its outer barriers and they sent a rapturous shudder across him, he probed in and in.

The kernel burst. That was no disaster, it was an unfolding. The atom embraced him, yielding to him, his being responded to her every least wild movement, he knew her. Radiance exploded outward. The morning stars sang together, and all the sons of God shouted for joy.

"Cosmology," said Joelle the omnipotent. He fumbled to find her in a toppling darkness. She enfolded him and they flew together, up a laser beam, through a satellite relay, to an observatory in orbit beyond the moon.

Briefly he spied the stars as if with his eyes, unblurred by any sky. Their multitudes, steel-blue, frost-white, sunset-gold, coal-red, well-nigh glittered the night out of heaven. The Milky Way rivered in silver, nebulae glowed where new suns and planets were being born, a sister galaxy flung her faint gleam across Ginnungagap. But at once he leagued with the instrumentality which was seeking the uttermost ends of space-time.

First he was aware of optical spectra. They told him of light that blossomed from leaping and whirling gas, they told him of tides in the body of a sun—a body more like the living cell than he could have imagined before—and of the furnaces down below where atoms begot higher elemental generations and photons racing spaceward were the birthcry. And in this Brahma-play he shared. Next he felt a solar wind blow past, he snuffed its richness, tingled to its keenness, and knew the millennial subtlety of its work. Thereafter he gave himself to radio spectra, cosmic ray spectra, magnetic fields, neutrino fluxes, relativistics which granted a star gate and seemed to grant time travel, the curve of the continuum that is the all.

At the Grand Canyon of the Colorado you may see strata going back a billion years, and across the view of them, a gnarly juniper, and know something of Earth. Thus did Eric learn something of the depths and the order in space-time. The primordial fireball became more real to him than the violence of his own birth, the question of what had brought it about became as terrifying. He bought the spirals of the galaxies and of the DNA molecule with energy which would never come back to him, and saw how the cosmos aged as it matured, even as you and I; the Law is One. He lived the lives of stars: how manifold were the waves that formed them, how strong the binding afterward to an entire existence! Amidst the massiveness of blue giants and black holes, he found room to forge planets whereon crystals and flowers could grow. He beheld what was still unknown—the overwhelming most of it, now and forever—and how Joelle longed to go questing.

Yet throughout, the observer part of him sensed that beside hers, his perception was misted and his understanding chained. When she drew him back to the flesh, he screamed.

They sat in the office. Her desk separated them. She had raised the blind on the window at her back and opened it. Shadows hastened across grass, sunlight that followed was bright but somehow as if the air through which it fell had chilled it, the gusts sounded hollow that harried smells of damp soil into the room, odors of oncoming autumn.

Though she spoke with much gentleness, her tone bore the same farewell to summer. "We couldn't have talked meaningfully before you'd been there yourself, could we have, Eric?"

His glance went to the empty couch. "How meaningful was anything between us, even at first?"

She sighed. "I wanted it to be." A smile touched her. "I did enjoy."

"No more than that, enjoy, eh?"

"I don't know. I do care for you, and for everything you taught me about. But I've gone on to, to where I tried to lead you."

"How far did I get?"

She stared down at her hands, folded on the desk in helplessness, and said low, "Still less than I feared. It was like showing a blind man a painting. He might get a tiny idea through his fingertips, texture, the dark colors faintly warmer than the light—but oh, how tiny!"

"Whereas you respond to the lot, from quanta to quasars," he rasped.

She raised her head, challenging their unhappiness. "No, I've barely begun, and of course I'll never finish. But don't you see, that's half of the wonder. Always more to find. Direct experience, as direct as vision or touch or hunger or sex, experience of the *real* reality. The whole world humans know is just a passing, accidental consequence of it. Each time I go to it, I know it better and it makes me more its own. How could I stop?"

"I don't suppose I could learn?"

Cherishing no hope, he was not surprised to hear: "No. A holothete has to start like me, early, and do hardly anything else, especially in those formative young years." He was touched when tears sprang into her eyes. So she did want to be his kin. "I'm sorry, darling. You're good and kind and . . . how I wish you could follow along. How you deserve it."

"You don't wish you could go back, though, to what you were when we met?"

"Would you?"

Unlinked, he could not truly summon up what had happened this day. His brain lay alone. Nevertheless— "No," he said. "In fact, I dare not ever try again. That could be addictive. For me, nothing but an addiction, and to lunacy. For you—" He shrugged. "Do you know the *Rubaiyat*?"

"I've heard of it," she said, "but I've had no chance to become cultured."

And will never take it, he thought while he recited the lines—

> "Why, if the Soul can fling the Dust aside,
> And naked on the Air of Heaven ride,
>   Were't not a Shame—were't not a Shame for
>   him
> In this clay carcase crippled to abide?"

—for human things will speak to you less and less, until finally you are not human yourself. Will you then be an Other, my dearest who was?

She nodded. "The old man told truth, didn't he? I did read once that Omar was a mathematician and astronomer. He must have been lonely."

"Like you, Joelle?"

"I have a few colleagues, remember. I'm teaching them—" She broke off, leaned across the desk, and said in a renewed concern: "What about us two? We'll be collaborating. You're strong enough to carry on, discharge your duty, I'm certain you are. But our personal lives—What's best for you?"

"Or for you?" he replied. "Let's take that up first."

"Anything you want, Eric," she said, "I'll gladly be your lover, wife, anything."

He was quiet a while, seeking words that might not hurt her. None came.

"You're telling me that you don't care which," he pronounced. "You're willing to treat me as well as

you're able, because it doesn't greatly matter to you."
He raised a palm to check her response. "Oh, no
doubt you'd get a limited pleasure from living with
me, even from my conversation. At the least, I'd help
fill in the hours when you can't be linked—until you
and those fellows of yours go so far that you'll have
no time for childish things."

"I love you," she protested. A pair of tears broke
loose.

He sighed. "I believe you. It's simply that love isn't
important any more, beside the grandeur. I've felt af-
fection for dogs I've kept. But—call it pride, prej-
udice, stubbornness, what you will—I can't play a
dog's part."

He rose. "We'll doubtless have an efficient partner-
ship till I go home," he ended. "Today, though, while
something remains of her, I'll tell my girl goodbye."

She sought him. He held her while she wept. It
might well be the last time in her life that she did.
When at length she kissed him, beneath a taste of
salt her lips were quite steady.

"Go back to your link for a bit," he counselled her.

"I will," she answered. "Thank you for saying it."

He walked out into a wind gone cold at evening.
She stood in the doorway and waved. He didn't turn
around to see, because he didn't want to know how
soon the door closed on her.